For Carl & Juli,
The Adventure Continues
Best to You Both,
KM Henderson
17 Nov 09

Brothers of the Forest

Ken Henderson

ISBN: 978-1-891029-22-6

Copyright 2005 by Ken Henderson

All rights reserved. Except for use in any review, the reproduction or utilization of this work, in whole or in part, in any form by electronic, mechanical or other means, now known or hereafter invented, including xerography, photocopying and recording, or any information storage or retrieval system is forbidden without the written permission of the author or his representative.

Second Printing

Cover design by the author.

You may contact the author at:
henpubs@4sw.us

See works by many other
Appalachian Authors at:
www.appalachianauthorsguild.com

HENDERSON PUBLISHING
811 Eva's Walk, Pounding Mill, VA 24637

About the Author

Ken Henderson, an avid early American history buff, lives in the beautiful mountains of Southwest Virginia, where the fictional home of Josh Mosby is located. Amid the scenery of the Appalachian Mountains, he has woven this early American adventure around the lives of several famous frontier legends who left their marks on the pages of history.

From his home in the Paintlick section of Tazewell County, he continues the adventures of Josh Mosby and his Seneca Indian friend, Tobahana, who were the main characters of his first novel, Painted Mountain.

Mr. Henderson and his wife, Marie, own Henderson Publishing, a small publishing company which produces six to eight new books each year for first-time authors looking to have their works published. He is retired from the U.S. Civil Service where he served as Chief of the Publications Division of U.S. Army Quartermaster College at Fort Lee, Virginia, producing training literature for the Army.

He is currently working with representatives of the Smithsonian Institute to preserve the ancient Indian paintings on Paintlick Mountain in Tazewell County. His effort in drawing attention to the mysterious paintings depicted in his first novel, has caused much interest in the preservation of the pictoglyphs.

His future plans include a third novel which will follow Josh Mosby and Tobahana as they choose to fight on the side of the colonists in the great Revolutionary War.

Mr. Henderson currently serves as Vice-Chairman of the Appalachian Authors Guild, which is devoted solely to assisting Appalachian writers promote their works.

*This book is dedicated to
Marie,
my wife and partner.*

Other Novels by Ken Henderson:

Painted Mountain - The beginning of Josh Mosby's journey to find a new home in the wilderness of the American Frontier in the 1750s. An adventure that will leave an indelible memory, based on actual people who survived the harsh times west of the Far Blue Mountains of Virginia.

Turning the Tide of War - To be published in 2007. The final book in the trilogy of this early American family. Join Josh Mosby as he becomes Chief of Scouts for the American Forces, culminating with the Battle of Kings Mountain. Follow the Overmountain Men as they prepare to meet the British in a battle that proved to be the turning point of the Revolutionary War in the South. An adventure with many twists and turns that it will keep the reader turning the pages.

TABLE OF CONTENTS

CHAPTER		PAGE
One	A Call to Duty	1
Two	Trouble Along the Frontier	11
Three	The Hunt	19
Four	Captured	29
Five	The Visitors	33
Six	A Cry for Death	41
Seven	Kentuckee	49
Eight	Tried in the Fire	61
Nine	A Visitor from the Past	65
Ten	On to Blue Lick	71
Eleven	Tana-qate	79
Twelve	Shawnee Justice	85
Thirteen	Timar's First Encounter	89
Fourteen	Answers Confirmed	97
Fifteen	Tobahana Speaks Out	103
Sixteen	A Plan to Escape	109
Seventeen	Tobahana's Trail	111
Eighteen	Trading Prisoners	119
Nineteen	TheFlight	131
Twenty	Timar Faces Death	137
Twenty One	Fight for Survival	145
Twenty-Two	Timar's Dilemma	155
Twenty-Three	End of the Trail	163
Twenty-Four	Telah's Story	171
Twenty-Five	Escape from Wolf River	179
	Epilogue	191

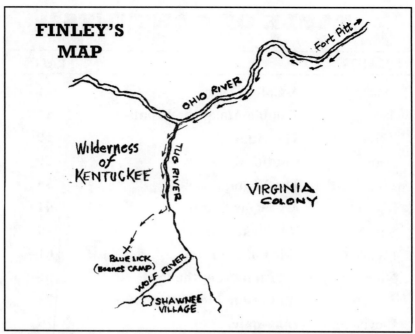
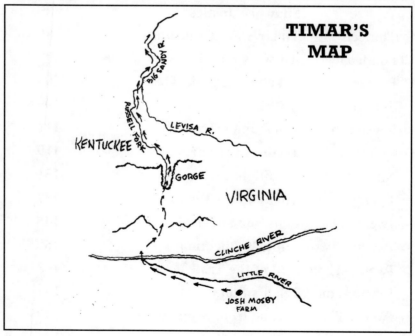

Chapter One
A Call To Duty

Tobahana could see the column of smoke rising from the little valley long before he reached the crest of the mountain north of Josh Mosby's small farm. He stood for a few minutes to catch his breath and reached into his pack for the brass spyglass to get a better view of the smoke's origin. Through the glass, he could make out the little farm nestled against the hillside several miles to the south. The smoke continued to rise in a long white plume from the place where his white friend made his home.

Thoughts of another Shawnee attack filled Tobahana's mind. Josh Mosby lost his family in an attack on his farm ten years ago, and now it looked as if it might be happening again. This time, it affected Tobahana; Josh was now his brother-in-law.

Josh and Meriah, Tobahana's sister, made their home in the little valley south of the Painted Mountain, where the Cherokee's once made their annual trek. The Cherokees allowed Josh to reclaim his farm and live there in peace in appreciation for his assistance in defeating the Shawnees. He and Meriah were married a year later by a traveling Presbyterian preacher, who stopped by the farm on his way to join settlers in Tennessee.

Tobahana was making his first visit to see his new niece, who was now two years old. Meriah, his only sister, was designated to become the leader of the Seneca tribe after the passing of their mother, but she chose to leave home to become the wife of his friend instead. She fell in love with Josh at Fort Pitt, while recuperating from a gunshot wound inflicted by Scarface, the Shawnee. Meriah and Timar, her young brother, refused to return to the Senecas and followed Tobahana and Josh south, eventually finding themselves at the Painted Mountain of the Cherokees. After the great battle between the Shawnee and Cherokee nations, she and Timar went to live with Josh on his farm in the foothills of the Clinche Mountains.

Tobahana ran as fast as his legs could carry him, hoping he would not be too late. Bounding over fallen tree trunks, racing through the thick underbrush, he wasted no time in getting down the mountain. He sped through the forest as nimble as a whitetail deer, and was soon across the little river which flowed a mile north of Josh's farm. In less than ten minutes, he came to the clearing near the cabin.

Stopping to catch his breath and survey the area, he checked the longrifle and primed the flintlock pistol in his belt. Laying aside his pack, Tobahana crept slowly toward the rear of the structure where the smoke continued to rise. He could see no movement inside or outside the cabin and concluded that he was too late to save anyone.

Suddenly, a shot rang from the cabin. Tobahana dove for cover behind the nearest tree stump and brought his rifle up, ready to fire on the first visible target. He lay behind the stump for several minutes, waiting for the next rifle ball to come.

While he lay concealed, he could see that the smoke did not come from the cabin, but rose from a pile of tree brush several yards from the back of the house. Relieved that the cabin was not in danger of burning, he knew he was mistaken about an attack on the farm. In fact, he had been mistaken as the attacker.

"Hello, the house!" Tobahana shouted. "It is Tobahana of the Senecas."

Immediately, the door of the little cabin opened and a tall man in buckskins stepped out. He carried a long flintlock rifle, which was lowered but still cocked, and looked toward the place from where the voice came.

"Step out and show yourself, Tobahana of the Senecas!" he shouted back.

A tall, graceful-looking Indian warrior rose from his hiding place and stood for a moment. He was dressed in tan buckskin breeches with blue and white trimmings on the sides. Over his broad shoulders, he wore a tight-fitting deerskin vest adorned with markings of the Seneca. Two eagle feathers were visible above the long, black hair that fell on his shoulders. Cradled in his strong arms was a long flintlock rifle, similar to the one he faced.

He spoke in the Seneca language, "It is good to see you again, Josh Mosby. I have traveled far this day to see my friend and his family."

He walked to where Josh stood on the porch of the little cabin and clasped the arm of his white brother. "I see smoke from long way and think you are attacked. I run fast only to find you are burning tree branches."

Josh held Tobahana's arm firmly while both men smiled at each other. "It is good to see you are still living. Meriah and I have waited for your visit. It has been a long while since we were on the trail together. I am glad you have finally come."

They stood their rifles against the wall of the cabin and Josh opened the door. "Meriah, we have company!" he shouted into the cabin.

The door to the bedroom opened and a beautiful dark-haired woman dressed in a long blue gingham dress came into the living room. Behind her, a small wide-eyed little girl peered from the folds of her mother's dress.

"Toba!" she shouted, and ran to the tall Indian who opened his arms and greeted his little sister in a warm embrace.

"You have not changed since we last saw you," Meriah said, with tears coming from her dark eyes. "We have looked for your visit almost every day. Josh said you would come, but I feared that something bad had happened to you."

"Much has happened since I see you and Josh. I will tell you about it later." Tobahana released Meriah and smiled at the small figure standing behind her.

"Who is this?" he asked jokingly, as the shy little girl peeked at him with wide eyes.

"This is your niece, Katherine Miskka Mosby. We call her Katy for short," said Meriah. She lifted little Katy and placed her in Tobahana's strong arms.

He took the child and held her at arm's length to admire his niece. He didn't have to ask where she got her middle name.

It was a name that he often recalled when he thought of the old Cherokee who had helped them escape from the French ship in Montreal. He approved of the thoughtfulness Josh and Meriah showed in giving her Miskka's name. He also knew how she got Katherine, her first name. It was the name of Josh's first wife, who had been massacred by the Shawnees nearly ten years ago.

At first, little Katy was reluctant to accept the stranger who held her so admiringly. She had been taught not to get too close to strangers who visited the farm, but this tall Indian seemed to be different than all the others. His warm smile and gentle touch made her feel comfortable.

"Hello, Katy," Tobahana said as he held her face to his. "I am Uncle Toba, your mother's brother. You are as beautiful as she was when she was your age." She smiled as he gave her a kiss on the cheek.

"I do not see Timar," Tobahana said, referring to his young brother who came to live with them on the farm.

"Timar is away with his new Cherokee friend, Sequah. They left two days ago to hunt in the mountains south of here. He should be returning soon," said Josh.

"You must be exhausted," said Meriah. "You have traveled far and I know you are hungry. I will prepare the evening meal while you and Josh talk." She and Katie left the men and went into the kitchen to start supper.

"I must get my pack which I left in the forest," said Tobahana.

"I'll go with you," replied Josh as he followed Tobahana outside. "We're glad to see you, Tobahana. It's been a long time."

They retrieved their rifles from the porch and walked toward the woods to retrieve Tobahana's pack. Both men were silent as they entered the forest. Each knew there would be time for talking when the evening meal was over.

Tobahana found the pack where he'd dropped it. He shouldered the heavy load and returned to where Josh waited.

As they walked back to the house, Josh proudly pointed to the cornfield which lay near the creek. "It's a good crop this year," he said, pointing to the five acres of ripening corn. "Each year I try to plant more, but it takes time to clear the land."

"Corn is good. Farm is good. Josh Mosby has done well," replied Tobahana.

When they reached the cabin, little Katy was standing on the porch waiting for them. She smiled as Tobahana sat the heavy pack down and began to open it.

He laid several articles of clothing aside and produced a small doeskin bag from the pack. Slowly, he untied the drawstring and reached his large brown hand inside and retrieved a string of beautiful lapiz azul beads. He could see the interest little Katy expressed as he pulled the necklace from the bag and smiled at her. She smiled back and lowered her head as if embarrassed.

Tobahana stretched out his hand and placed the necklace around Katy's neck. "This is present for Tobahana's favorite niece," he said.

With wide eyes and a huge smile, Katie ran quickly to show her mother the present Uncle Toba had given her.

The meal was the best Tobahana had tasted and kept telling Meriah how much he enjoyed it. She had prepared a venison pot roast, with Irish potatoes, carrots and onions simmered in the same pot. A large pone of cornbread, served with fresh butter, topped off the main course. Fresh sassafras tea and hot blackberry cobbler was served for dessert.

Tobahana ate until he could no longer swallow another bite. "Good! Now, I know why Josh marry you," he laughed and drained the last of the tea from his glass.

He thanked Meriah again for the meal and he and Josh retired to the chairs on the front porch.

Josh pulled a pouch of tobacco from his shirt pocket, stuffed the bowl of his pipe and offered the pouch to Tobahana. Tobahana declined the offer and Josh called for Katy to bring him a light. In a moment, she came out, holding a firebrand in her small hands. Josh lit the pipe and blew out the fire from the end of the match.

"I come with news from Fort Pitt," Tobahana said as they settled into the wooden chairs. "Big things happen all along the frontier. New British colonel at Fort Pitt is much worried about news of fight between colonials and English king. He say big fight is coming that no one can stop.

I hear with my own ears that many people are angry with King George and his regulations. White settlers now come to Ohio country in great numbers to escape king's new demand for tax on all citizens. Most colonials do not heed king's proclamation that say no English will go beyond Blue Mountains. Many people come down great rivers to Fort Pitt and settle in Indian country."

Josh could see the worry in Tobahana's eyes as he continued. "Not many moons past, I hear news of English soldiers and colonials in big fight in Boston City. Soldiers kill two citizens and cause much trouble. People who live in Boston City very angry and want English to leave. Commandant at Fort Pitt say it is beginning of much trouble along frontier. He very worried."

Josh responded, "I've also heard that there is unrest in the east. Many travelers who pass on their way west, tell me that they're fed up with the way things are in the colonies and have no respect for the British."

"I have also seen many travelers come down two rivers that form Ohio. Most have all they own with them and will never return to be ruled by English," said Tobahana. "That is part of why I come to see you and Meriah. There will be much anger from Indians who live west of Blue Mountains. They will fight to keep their land."

Josh listened closely as Tobahana told him about the other reason for his visit.

"Colonel Bouquet is no longer at Fort Pitt. A new English colonel now in charge. He is very interested in enlisting help from settlers west of Blue Mountains. He say, they should stick together with English and fight against Shawnee raiders who cause much trouble along whole frontier," Tobahana said.

He continued, "New colonel is good man. He want peace with all Indian tribes and want me to help stop renegade Shawnees who kill innocent women and children. I tell him I will help only if my friend Josh Mosby help also. He say, go see Josh Mosby and tell him to come to fort. That is big reason why Tobahana is here."

Josh looked into the eyes of his old friend. "I know many settlers are now clearing land and building homes all along the frontier. I have seen many families pass by the farm each month, on their way west to the rich farmland in Tennessee. I have also seen many come back because they lost family members in Indian attacks on their homes. It's a terrible thing to lose everything you've worked so hard to build. Believe me, I know how it feels to lose your family to savages."

He fought back tears as he tried to keep the scene of his first family's deaths out of his mind. Ten years ago, he watched the Shawnees murder his wife and two little boys as he lay beaten and unable to stop them. Josh Mosby swore to avenge their deaths, and although he and Tobahana succeeded in killing those responsible, the memories of that terrible day still lingered.

Josh was sure that many other families had experienced the same tragedy and he prayed that he would never go through it again. He almost lost his will to live in the Shawnee prison camp and probably would have died there, had it not been for his good friend, Tobahana, who was also imprisoned with him. His mind drifted back to hear what Tobahana was saying.

"Colonel Webster say if you come to fort and sign contract, he will pay good money for good scout. He need many frontier men who know forest and lay of land west of Blue Mountains. He say Shawnee raids have to be stopped and only way is to hire good scouts to find bad Shawnee and report to him," Tobahana spoke.

He continued, "You have scouted Shawnee country with me. I do not trust anyone else. I tell colonel that I will take scout job only if you will come."

Josh could see the concern in Tobahana's face, but he

couldn't see any way that he could leave the farm and his family to take a scouting job that would take him away from home for many months. The crops would be ready to harvest within a couple of months and preparations for the coming winter had to be done. Firewood had to be cut and stored, meat for the smokehouse had to be hunted and cured, and the cabin needed repairs before the snows of winter fell.

He also hated the thought of leaving Meriah and Katy with only Timar to watch over them. Although Timar was now a strong man of twenty-three years, he was young and headstrong and apt to make many wrong decisions during the coming winter. Josh had taught Timar the ways of the white man during his stay on the farm, and he finally consented to having his hair cut short and wear the same clothing as Josh.

Timar now resembled a white settler more than a Seneca warrior. He had been with Josh and his sister since the big fight with the Shawnees at Painted Mountain nearly ten years ago. Only once had he left the farm, and that was on a trip with two of his Cherokee friends to Ken-tuck-ee to hunt buffalo. Meriah worried about her little brother day and night until he returned.

Josh was now faced with a problem. He could not leave the farm and go on the trail with Tobahana. Yet, he owed it to Tobahana, who had saved his life on numerous occasions. He would undoubtedly be dead, or wasting away as a slave to the Shawnees or some other Indian tribe had it not been for Tobahana.

"How soon are you going back on the trail?" asked Josh.

"That will depend on when you can leave with me," said Tobahana.

"There is just no way that I can go with you at this time. Without preparation, I doubt if Meriah and Katy would make it through the winter. Timar is a great help, but I don't think he can get everything layed by before cold weather comes." Josh pointed to the cornfield. "Besides, the corn is not ready to harvest and we will need it to live on during the coming winter."

"Then we will go when the corn is gathered," said Tobahana. "I will stay and help. We will leave when everything is done."

"I appreciate your offer to help, but I still will not be able to go without Meriah's blessing, and she will be very hard to convince," said Josh.

"I will convince Meriah," replied Tobahana. "We will not tell her about our trip until later. She will understand."

"We'll see," chuckled Josh.

Looking toward the cornfield, they saw three heads bobbing through the green rows of tall corn. Tobahana reached for his longrifle as Josh stood and waved. "It's Timar and his friends."

Three young men burst through the corn and came to a dead stop when they saw Josh and Tobahana standing on the cabin porch. At once, Timar recognized Tobahana and raced to meet his older brother. In his haste, he failed to see the clothesline that stretched between the two trees in the front yard. He hit the line about neck high and went sprawling, sending his rifle and pack flying into the air, landing on his back with the breath knocked from his lungs. Tobahana and Josh let out a loud whoop of laughter as Timar scrambled to his feet and ran forward.

"Toba! Toba! I knew you would be coming," he said as he reached the porch and embraced Tobahana with a big bear hug.

"You now a grown warrior," said Tobahana, grasping Timar's shoulders, admiring the stature of his young brother. "Long time since we see each other. You grow tall like me."

He released his young brother as Meriah and Katy came out of the house

"He is now a full grown warrior of Senecas," said Tobahana to his sister and Josh. "You raise him well. I am glad Timar stay with you."

"He's been a big help. We're glad he stayed with us. Timar and Josh are like brothers and get along well together. Sometimes, I believe they know what the other is thinking," said Meriah.

Timar introduced his Cherokee friends to Tobahana.

"Toba, meet my hunting partners, Sequah and Menah. They are here with a large Cherokee hunting party which comes north to hunt every year. They have been my friends for three summers."

The young Cherokees stepped forward and grasped Tobahana's forearm. Sequah spoke for both, "Timar speaks much of the great warrior who kills our enemy, the Shawnee. Many times he tell story of great fight between Tobahana and Scarface. We are honored to meet such a warrior."

Tobahana tried not to show his pride for what his little brother had told his friends about him. "I fight many times with Scarface, but was never able to kill him. Another great warrior stands before you," he said, pointing to Josh Mosby, his brother-in-law.

"Tobahana owes his life to this man who kill Scarface," he said. "Josh Mosby is called White Eagle among the Senecas. He very good with longrifle, kill many Shawnee."

The young Cherokees were surprised at what Tobahana said. It was hard for them to believe that this white farmer, who seemed so out of place on the frontier, was capable of killing anyone, much less Scarface, the hated Shawnee. Perhaps they would be more respectful to this quiet man who lived among the Cherokees.

Sequah and Menah bade farewell to Timar and the others and disappeared into the forest. They would have quite a story to tell when they got back to camp.

Meriah called the men to the supper meal at the close of the evening. Again, Tobahana remarked about how good the food was as she took special care to see that his plate stayed full. When the meal was over, the three men sat on the porch and talked until darkness fell on the little valley.

Chapter 2
Trouble Along the Frontier

Amos Boggs' buckskin clothes were well-soaked as he stumbled through the downpour on the cobblestone street leading past the circular brick armory in Williamsburg. He was already two hours late for his appointment with the governor's adjutant, but he didn't seem to let it bother him. The stench of sweaty body odor, escaping through his buckskin blouse, left a trail that caused people to avoid him and pass on the opposite side of the street.

During the previous evening at the Boar's Head Tavern, Boggs drank and caroused with the regular patrons until closing time. With no place to sleep, he talked the proprietor into letting him bed down beneath the tavern's rear stairwell. It was well past his appointment time when he awoke to find that it was still raining. He gathered his wet belongings, picked up his longrifle and found his way toward the main street, leading to the governor's mansion.

Colonel James Beecham, Adjutant for Governor Dinwiddie, rose from his huge oak desk and extended a hand to the buckskin-clad visitor. Boggs, who stood looking at the huge portraits of King George and Governor Dinwiddie on the wall behind the desk, took the small smooth-skinned hand of his host and gave it a hearty squeeze.

"Please have a seat, Mr. Boggs," he said, pointing to the tall leather-backed chair in front of his desk.

Boggs removed his shabby black tri-corn hat and laid the flintlock on the floor beside the chair. He brushed off the seat with his dirty hand and sat facing the colonel.

"I guess you're wondering why I've sent all the way to Fort Chiswell for you?" he asked, hoping for a pleasant reply from Boggs.

"Yeah," said the frontiersman. "I jist spent the better part of a week gittin' here. Would'na come 'cept'n Capt'n Wilson's holdin' three months pay 'til I git back. Wouldn't pay me 'less I come to see ye first."

"Captain Wilson is a good soldier. He had orders from the governor to release your pay only if you come to Williamsburg." The adjutant took his seat and opened a scroll of maps, spreading them neatly across the top of his desk.

"Mr. Boggs, I want to show you why you're here," he said, motioning for the smelly scout to look at the map.

"I'm sure you're aware of the Indian troubles on the western frontier. There's been a number of raids on the white settlements all along the border," he said, as he pointed to several points on the large map.

Boggs rose and leaned over the desk to take note of the raid sites. Colonel Beecham continued, "Your area around Fort Chiswell has been no exception. The raiders seem to be hitting at random. We don't know where they'll hit next." He put a finger on the map and moved it southward, stopping at a point near the border of North Carolina.

"From the Ohio, south to the New and Holston Rivers, they seem to know where to hit and do the most damage. Our forts in the west have all been alerted with orders to protect our citizens, but we don't have the manpower to protect everyone," he said, as he touched a straw to candle and lit his clay pipe while Boggs scanned the map. After a few puffs, he laid it in a glass tray and continued.

"We are recruiting several scouts, such as you, Mr. Boggs, to help us find the source of these raids. If we can identify the Indians responsible for these atrocities, and capture the leader, then we can concentrate our forces and eliminate the problem." The colonel retrieved the smoldering pipe and drew on the stem until the bowl glowed to life again.

Boggs took a few minutes to examine the map more closely. Then, he placed a finger on the map and tapped. "This here is where I would bet the head varmit is located. See how the places they've been hittin' are within a hunnert miles or so of this location?"

He stepped back so the colonel could take a closer look and continued, "That's why it looks like random raids. They're hittin' within this hunnert-mile circle. My guess is that their main camp is somewhere near the center."

The colonel was impressed with Boggs' rationale. "By Jove, I think you're right! Looks like all the raids within the past few months fall within a hundred miles of this location." He tapped the area on the map with his pipe.

After several minutes of deliberation, the colonel resumed his conversation. "Mr. Boggs, I want you to scout this area and report your findings to the commander at Fort Chiswell. I will see to it that an extra month's wages await you when you get back to the fort. Captain Wilson will relay your findings to me when you report to him."

"I reckon I can do that," said Boggs. He took the opportunity to ask for several things before leaving the adjutant's office. "I'll need a pack horse and supplies before I leave. Maybe a new rifle and enough shot and powder to see me through the next few months."

Colonel Beecham scribbled a few lines on a piece of stationary. "Take this note to the armory and they will give you what supplies you need. Tell them you'll be needing a pack horse to carry the supplies when you leave town."

The colonel shook hands with Boggs and bade farewell to the frontiersman. Boggs stuffed the note into his pocket and retrieved his rifle from the floor. He started to ask another favor of the adjutant, but decided a keg of ale would be pressing his luck. He doffed his shabby tri-corn and left the office.

The dappled gray pack horse, loaded with a new supply of equipment and food, followed the lead horse with its rider down the western side of the blue mountain range. For nearly a week, they had traversed the ridges and valleys, guided by the rank smelling human that cursed and urged them onward. At sundown, the rider led them down into a large cavern on the western side of the mountain. The entrance to the cavern was wide enough to allow both horses ample room to enter, and the man wasted no time unloading the horses.

Amos Boggs camouflaged the entrance to the cave with tree branches to keep the horses inside and visitors out. He picked up his shoulder pack and rifle and left the area of the cavern. Boggs looked back at the hidden entrance several times before he was satisfied that it couldn't be seen. Although anyone knowing its location would have no trouble finding it, he hoped to return before it was discovered.

Boggs headed west, toward the New River, which ran through a wide valley, nearly a day's journey from the cavern. Twice, he came upon Indian sign and went several miles out of his way to avoid being seen. He knew several Shawnee hunting parties used the trails east of the river, and without careful attention, a man could loose his hair.

His plan was to cross the river and check with the commandant at Fort Chiswell before returning for his horses and equipment. Traveling without the two horses left a much easier trail to cover. With all the Indian activity in the area, Boggs needed to be wary. A broken twig or footprint left uncovered could mean discovery, or worse, he could be taken prisoner by the hated Shawnees.

He reached the New River just as the sun cast its last rays across the western hills within few miles of Fort Chiswell. He hoped to cross the river under cover of darkness to lessen the chance of being seen. The ferry, which was operated during daylight hours, was making its final crossing when he arrived at the small building on the eastern side of the river.

Old Jake Wilson pulled the wooden ferry boat against its mooring station and tossed the tie-down rope to Amos, who caught the rope and threw it over the worn stump and pulled it fast. Wilson hobbled off the ferry and shook hands with the traveler.

"Too late to cross today. Just made the last trip," said Old Jake. "Won't be on the river agin' 'til daylight."

"Don't plan to use yer ferry. I'm goin' across later tonight," said Boggs.

Old Jake checked the mooring line to be sure the ferry was securelly tied and motioned toward the shack. "You can stay the night here if you've a mind to. Won't be makin' the next run 'til daybreak."

Boggs was not ready to cross the river, so he followed Old Jake into the small shack and seated himself on a wooden keg, which he pulled upright. The old man scurried around the small room, found the misplaced poker and stoked the fire to life in the black pot-bellied stove. Later, over a briming cup of hot English tea, the old man and Amos Boggs conversed about the traffic on the river, and about Indian activity in the area.

"Ain't been much notice of Indians hereabouts. Guess it's 'cause the fort's just acrost the river. But, I did see a couple of canoes 'tother evenin' just about dusk. They was headin' north 'long the far side of the river. Couldn't make out who they was. Shawnee, I suppose," Old Jake remarked.

"Wal, they best not be stoppin' on the river," replied Boggs. "The commandant over to Fort Chiswell don't know it yet, but he's about to be more active in Injun affairs hereabouts."

He reached into his buckskin overshirt and produced a leather tobacco pouch. After filling his clay pipe, he offered the pouch to Old Jake, who graciously accepted. Boggs retrieved a sliver of wood from the wood bin and touched it to the pot-bellied stove and it flamed to life. He drew on the pipe until the tobacco glowed red, and then handed the hot splinter to Old Jake.

"Reckon ye've heered 'bout all the Injun raids on the settlers 'round here," said Boggs. "I've been plumb to Williamsburg to find out 'bout it. Seems like they know more back east than we do out here on the frontier."

"Wal, I did heer of a raid on some settlers twenty miles to the north, a week or so ago, but didn't heer who done it. 'Spect it was them blasted Shawnee renegades." Old Jake took a few puffs from his pipe and continued. "Seems a whole family was massacred. They didn't have a chance. Them stinkin' Injuns even murdered the young'uns."

"Reckon they're part of the trouble goin' on 'round here.

I fear we ain't seed the last of them varmits," replied Boggs.

The scout thumped his pipe against the stove, knocking out the remaining hot coals, and picked up an old woolen blanket from the pile of smelly bedding lying on the floor of the shack. He cleared a spot in the corner of the shack and made a bed.

"Wake me up in a couple hours."

Old Jake grunted a reply and left the shack to Boggs. He walked down to where the ferry was docked and checked the mooring lines before calling it a day. As he looked out across the fast moving water of the New, he wondered what was so important to Boggs that he couldn't wait until tomorrow to cross the river.

Old Jake didn't hear the rank-smelling visitor leave. He awakened around midnight to see that Boggs and his gear were gone. There was something about the man that caused him to say, "Good riddance!", under his breath as he recovered the blanket Boggs had used, and spread it across his own bed.

In the early morning hours before sunrise, Boggs made his way across the river. He carried his clothes and rifle over his head as he waded ashore several hundred yards downstream from the ferry. The crossing was not nearly as hard as he thought it would be. He waded the shallows between several small islands and only had to swim across two narrow stretches of the fast moving water.

Within a few minutes, he donned his smelly buckskins and soon regained the body warmth he'd lost in the frigid water. After pulling on his worn boots, Boggs checked his rifle and possibles pouch to see if everything was still dry. Satisfied that his powder and equipment had survived the crossing without water damage, he left the river and made his way toward Fort Chiswell.

"Hello, the gate!" Boggs shouted as he walked up to the palisade surrounding the small fort.

He heard a bustle of activity within the walls and soon the large wooden gate swung open. An armed guard, dressed in the familiar British red coat and white trousers, extended a greeting to the early morning visitor.

"Well, well. I see you finally decided to grace us with your presence," said the guard, as he snapped a sarcastic salute and granted passage to Boggs.

Without replying, the scout brushed past the guard and made his way toward the commandant's quarters on the far side of the palisade. The fort was just coming to life. He noticed several soldiers, still half dressed on the barrack porch, shaving and washing their faces in pans of warm water. Steam rose from the dirty water tossed onto the ground, as each man finished his morning task.

Boggs rapped loudly upon the door of the commandant's quarters and was answered by Captain Wilson himself.

"Glad to see you back, Boggs," said the commandant, admitting the scout to his office. "Have a seat and tell me about your trip."

Boggs propped his longrifle against the doorframe and walked over to the chair facing the commandant's desk. "T'aint much to tell. I met with the adjutant just like ye ordered," he said, taking a cigar from the box on the desk.

Taking time to bite off the end of the cigar and light it with a piece of wood from the fireplace, Boggs continued, "He seems more aware of the Injun trouble out here than we do. Says that there's big Injun trouble right here in our neck of the woods."

"What else did Colonel Beecham tell you?" asked Captain Wilson.

"Said he can't send any troops 'til we locate the source of the trouble. 'Cordin' to the colonel, there's been a lot of Injun raids on settlers jist north of us. He wants me to scout the territory and find out who's stirrin' up the Injuns." Boggs leaned back in the chair and blew cigar smoke across the desk.

"I wondered why the adjutant specifically requested our best scout to come to Williamsburg. Did you tell him you would help find the responsible party?" asked the captain.

"Wal, I didn't say I wouldn't. Told him you're holdin' my pay 'til I got back and he said he'd pay me an extry six months wages 'iffin' I found out who is doin' the raidin'." Boggs lied about the promised extra wages.

"Good," said Captain Wilson. "Then I expect to see you on the trail by sunrise tomorrow."

"Can't go anywhere without gittin' outfitted. Lost my rig and horse, tryin' to git 'em across last night," lied Boggs again. "Guess you can 'ford me another horse and pack mule 'fore I hit the trail again."

"Man, why in heaven didn't you take the ferry across the river?" asked the captain. "Seems like a big waste, knowing the danger of crossing a river that has claimed several lives already."

"I was in a hurry," replied Boggs. "'Sides, Old Jake shut down the ferry 'fore he could git me across last night. Figured I'd already wasted enough time lookin' fer Injun sign east of the river."

The captain threw up his hands and paced back and forth across the room. "I just can't understand why you couldn't wait until today to cross the river. You know good horses are hard to come by out here on the frontier."

"Wal, the milk has done been spilt," retorted Boggs, "Can't do no more scoutin' 'less I git reoutfitted."

Captain Wilson tried to regain his composure and stopped pacing. Still upset, he pointed a shaking finger at the scout. "I expect you on the trail at first light tomorrow. Go by the stables and pick out a horse and mule. Then, see the quartermaster and draw supplies. At least you haven't lost your rifle. I will be waiting on your report within a week."

"Ye wouldn't mind if I collected my back pay 'fore I go, would ye, Capt'n?"

Captain Wilson threw up his hands, thoroughly disgusted with Boggs. He scribbled a quick note on paper and handed it to the scout without another word.

Boggs could see he was no longer welcome in the captain's quarters. He sauntered outside, grabbing his rifle as he left. "Guess I'll see if I can find me a drink," he said, and walked toward the troop barrack.

Chapter Three
The Hunt

Meriah knew what Josh was going to ask long before he came to bed. In the years since their marriage, she had grown to love this gentle man so much, that she could anticipate his requests and actions with such accuracy that it amazed him.

She also knew Tobahana. It did not take a miracle to figure out why he had come. Meriah knew his excuse to visit Katy was his way to see Josh again, and she was afraid.

"We need to talk about some things," said Josh, as he climbed into the bed and nestled closely to Meriah.

"I expect it has something to do with Toba's visit, doesn't it?" she replied.

"Yes, it does, but it depends on what your answer will be when I finish telling you what he wants," replied Josh.

He was silent for several minutes as he tried to find the words to explain the importance of Toba's visit. During their nearly ten years of marriage, he and Meriah had openly expressed their true feelings when it came to making decisions. Yet, as he lay next to the woman he loved, he was torn between his desire to go on the trail with Tobahana and his duty to stay with his family.

Josh knew it would be dangerous on the frontier trail and there was a possibility he would never return to the little farm. He also knew what faced Meriah and Katy during the harsh winter months that would surely bring hardships. Timar would be a great help to Meriah and would lay down his life to protect her and his little niece, but he was young and lacked experience.

He searched for the words to explain the importance of Tobahana's visit, knowing that if he were to go back on the trail, it would be due to Meriah's answer, and he was afraid.

"Tobahana wants me to go with him to Fort Pitt to talk to the new commandant. He said the commandant needs our help to locate the source of Indian trouble along the border. You know how much the colonel depended on Tobahana and me when we arranged the treaty with the Shawnee, and I fear that if we don't help him get to the bottom of the attacks on the farms and villages here on the frontier, there will be no end to the destruction." Josh said, as he sat up and swung his feet off the bed.

When he had sat there for a time, he felt the touch of Meriah's hand on his shoulder. "My heart feels the tearing in my husband's heart. I know that Toba is here on important business. Otherwise, he would not have come for your help."

"Then, your heart knows what I'm trying to say," replied Josh. "It has been a long time since we were on the trail of Scarface. I don't know if I would be able to make it out there on the trail again. I fear that I'll let Tobahana down."

"Toba would not have made the long trip from Fort Pitt if he thought you'd let him down. He has faith in you, my husband," said Meriah. "You and Toba are more than brothers of the forest; you are brothers of the heart."

"My greatest fear is leaving you and little Katy alone this winter. If I go, I know we won't be coming back for a few months, and I'm afraid Timar is too young to face the problems that winter will bring," said Josh.

He knew that his Cherokee friends would stop in frequently to check on them, but if the winter was harsh, they might not come. Josh also knew of the dangers from the north. The Shawnees were still causing much havoc with their occasional raids on area settlers. His nearest neighbor was more than twenty-five miles away and would not be able to help if the Shawnees struck his farm.

During the years since their marriage, he had taught Meriah much about defending herself and the baby. Her willingness to learn how to handle the flintlock rifle and pistol made him feel confident that she could protect herself, but he was still uncomfortable about leaving little Katy and her, with only Timar to protect them.

"You don't have to worry about us," said Meriah. "We have been able to get through the last ten years without trouble.

Besides, our friends, the Cherokee, will see that we are protected. I think that is why we have been able to live here in peace all these years."

"I will send Timar to talk to the Cherokees before it is time for us to leave," said Josh, feeling somewhat better about leaving. "He can tell them why I am going. They will understand the importance of bringing the Shawnee raids under control."

"See, my husband, it is not as bad as it seems," replied Meriah.

"I guess I worry too much. I am still not convinced that you'll be safe, but if the Cherokees will promise to watch over the farm, I will feel much better. They will be camping for the winter at the Elk Garden hunting grounds south of here, so maybe they will not mind to drop in on you occasionally. Besides, it's only right since they will be coming for their share of the corn and dried vegetables we've raised," said Josh.

"You can tell Toba that you will be going with him," said Meriah. "We'll be fine until you return."

Josh climbed back under the covers and pulled Meriah close to him. "You know that I love you and little Katy more than anything else in the world. Thank you for being so understanding. If I didn't think the trip was important, I would tell Tobahana to go on alone."

- - -

The summer flew by with the warm breezes that flowed across the little valley. Autumn followed, with an early mountain snow during the first week of November, keeping the men inside for several days. When the snow melted, warmer days followed and the harvest and woodcutting resumed.

With three men in the fields, the work of harvesting and storing the corn, beans, and potatoes went smoothly. The small storehouse was filled to overflowing with the bountiful harvest, with more than enough to share with the Cherokees.

Satisfied that his crops were stored away for the winter, Josh spoke to Tobahana and Timar. "Now, we can go on a hunt to put some meat in the smokehouse. I told Meriah we would see to it before we left."

Timar was pleased to be going hunting with his older brother, who had never seen his skill with a rifle. He knew the surrounding mountain ranges like the back of his hand and also knew where the largest herd of elk and whitetail deer grazed. The hunt would be the perfect time to show his expertise with the new flintlock rifle Josh had given him.

On the night before the hunt, Timar cleaned and oiled his rifle over and over, until Tobahana, who was watching, said, "Little brother, if you shine rifle much more, you will have no sights left."

Embarrassed, Timar quickly gathered up his equipment and sauntered off to his bed. That night, he dreamed of shooting elk and deer until he was awakened by Tobahana, who spent the night on the floor beside the bed.

"We ready to go now. Do you plan to sleep all day?" Tobahana joked.

"I'll be ready in a minute," replied Timar, jumping to his feet, quickly donning the buckskins he laid out the night before.

In his haste, he stumbled over the longrifle he'd propped against the bed. The noise of the gun hitting the wooden floor echoed throughout the cabin, waking Meriah and little Katy, who came running out of their room.

"What was that noise?" said Katy, clinging to her mother's night gown.

"Your Uncle Timar just wanted to let everyone know that he's about to go hunting," laughed Josh. He continued to laugh at his brother-in-law, "Remember the last time when he fell off the porch and shot a hole through the roof?"

Everyone laughed except Timar, who silently closed the bedroom door.

"I might as well fix breakfast for you hunters since I'm awake," said Meriah, still smiling about Timar's latest blunder.

After a filling breakfast of fresh eggs, healthy cuts of fried deer loin and biscuits, the hunters bade farewell to Meriah and

Katy. They made their way southward, along the crest of Clinche Mountain to the head of a small valley, just as dawn broke in the eastern skies. It was here that Josh always began his fall hunt.

A small stream tumbled off the mountain, wound it's way through the mountain laurel thickets, and trickled on down the little valley. The thick mountain laurel gave way to an open forest of huge oak, poplar and chestnut trees. Here, the elk came to gorge on the abundant crop of sweet chestnuts and acorns that covered the forest floor. The fattening chestnuts also drew the whitetail, black bear, and an occasional buffalo to feed in the little valley.

Later in the season, the Cherokees would be arriving to spend the winter months hunting the bountiful game in the valley they called Elk Garden. They would be camping on the headwaters of Little Cedar Creek, two miles from where Josh and his party were now located.

The friendly Cherokees always made a visit to his farm to collect their tribute, which consisted of corn, potatoes, and dried beans. It was never a great amount, but they were glad to receive anything that the Mosby's gave them. Occasionally, Meriah would include fresh herbs and dried fruit, which always pleased the grateful Cherokee visitors. They also brought fine furs of otter, mink, and red fox to trade for Meriah's handsomely decorated buckskin vests and leggings.

Occasionally, Meriah would give them a special treat of maple syrup if the season for gathering maple sap in the nearby mountain had been good. She also took special pride in having enough butter to share with her Cherokee friends, who always accepted the treats with smiles to show their gratitude.

Timar, who was anxious to show his big brother that he was now a warrior and hunter, volunteered to be the driver on the hunt. He left Josh and Tobahana at the upper end of the cove and made his way along the ridge to the south, making sure to conceal himself from the elk and deer in the valley below. Within an hour, he was ready to begin the drive up the valley toward his fellow hunters.

Tobahana had never hunted game in this way. He had always stalked his prey and was most successful in his hunting trips. He could see the benefit of of having the game driven to him, but couldn't understand why Josh and Timar would give up the fun of the stalk. After considering the method, he concluded that it was the best way to put meat on Josh's table.

They made their stand behind fallen timbers about a hundred yards apart and waited for Timar to begin his drive. Each of them laid out their powderhorn, along with extra shot, so they could reload as fast as possible. The elk and whitetails would be coming up the valley on a dead run, straight for the mountain laurel thickets behind them.

Little more than an hour later, they could hear Timar blowing the buffalo horn, signaling them that he was beginning the drive. They hunkered down in the concealing brush to await the oncoming game.

Several minutes later, four whitetails, with their flags waving, broke into the open in front of Josh's position. Since he could see they were yearling does, he let them go by and remained hidden. Minutes later, a large bull elk, with his head in the air, came into view. The elk came on toward them and suddenly stopped, as if he detected something in front of him. His nostrils flared and he bellowed a loud shrill as if to warn those following him.

As he ended the warning, Tobahana fired from fifty yards away. The bull elk raised his head one more time but no sound came. Only the echo of the rifle shot reverberated through the forest. He fell right where he stood, taking the ball just behind his right ear. Tobahana waved to Josh, who motioned for him to stay put.

During the next hour, Josh and Tobahana killed another elk and three whitetail bucks, all falling within a few yards of the first elk. Josh moved out of his hiding place and motioned for Tobahana to follow him. They moved toward the fallen game just as Timar came into view.

"Looks like we got them," Timar said, as he rushed toward them. In his arms, he carried a small black bear cub. "Found this little fellow in a hollow log not far from here."

Tobahana recognized the danger first. Behind Timar came a huge black bear, dashing straight for her captured cub. Before he could get into a position to shoot the bear, it slammed into Timar, taking him and the bear cub down, sprawling on all fours. Instantly, the mother bear was on top of the young Indian, raking her sharp claws across his back. He released the cub and it scampered into the forest, emitting a loud cry of freedom.

Over and over Timar and the old sow rolled, breaking down saplings and bushes as they fought. Josh and Tobahana stood helplessly by, unable to take a shot for fear of hitting Timar, who had his hands full of mad bear.

As suddenly as it began, it was all over. Timar managed to get to his hunting knife, and with a lucky thrust, he found the huge bear's heart. She rolled off him, kicked a few times and lay still. The young Indian, torn and mangled, managed to get to his feet and looked down at the huge form of the mother bear.

With blood running down his face, he grinned at his older brother, who smiled back and said, "The spirits have been with you, my brother. You are fortunate to be standing. I have seen many strong braves sent to the spirit world by a mother black bear."

Josh joined them and said, "You are very lucky, Timar. You should have known better than take a cub from its mother."

Timar felt both proud and ashamed at the same time. He had been told by Josh on many hunting trips to beware of just such an incident. In his haste to impress Tobahana, he had made a terrible mistake that almost cost him his life.

His clothing hung in shreds and blood oozed from the claw marks on his back. He stood with knife still in hand as if in a trance and stared at the mound of black hair beside him. Tobahana walked to him and took the bloody knife from his hand.

"I'm sorry," said Timar. "I knew better. I just wanted to show you the bear cub. I promised Katy that I'd bring her a pet and I thought the cub would please her."

"I'm sure Katy would have been pleased, but did you think of the problems in raising a bear cub?" asked Josh. "Why, in a couple of years, the cub will be near the size of its mother."

"I guess I never thought much about that," replied Timar, hanging his head. "I just didn't think."

"Well, we've got another problem now. The cub has no mother and will die here in the forest if we don't find it," said Tobahana. "I'll track it and bring it back while you help Josh. But first, let us take care of your wounds."

The bear left several long claw wounds on Timar's back. He sat motionless while Tobahana and Josh cleaned and bound them. The wounds were not life-threatening, but would become infected without proper care.

Josh fetched water from the creek and washed the blood from around the wounds. From his pack, he produced a flask of corn whisky that he carried just for such an accident and doused Timar's back. The alcohol burned like fire as it ran into the open claw marks, but Timar showed no sign of pain. When he had wrapped the wounds with pieces of Timar's torn shirt, they sat and waited on Tobahana to return.

An hour later, Tobahana returned with the black bear cub tucked under his arm. "I chased him up a tree and caught him," he said. "This little rascal gave me quite a round. Bit me three times when I tried to corner him."

"Well, I guess we're stuck with him until we can figure out what to do with him," said Josh. "I guess Katy will be getting her pet after all."

With the bear cub securely tied to a tree with a rawhide leash, the three of them spent the next several hours butchering their kill. Only the choicest cuts were taken, since carrying the fresh meat back to the farm was a dreaded task. The meat that couldn't be carried was wrapped in the black bearskin and hoisted into a nearby tree for safekeeping until they could return for it.

Tobahana fashioned two travois from tall saplings and lashed down the elk and deer hams. When the load was secured, they began the back-breaking trip back to the farm. The trek took them several miles out of the way, but it kept them from hauling their loads back across the mountain. He and Josh pulled the loaded travois while Timar carried their longrifles and pulled the leashed bear cub along behind him. It was long past sundown when they saw the light at Josh's cabin.

Meriah and Katy met them as they crossed the little stream which flowed by their home. In the darkness, they had waited at the ford until they heard the men coming up the valley trail. They were glad the hunters were back and they had important news to tell them.

Timar was the first to cross the creek, pulling the bear cub along behind. He proudly presented Katy with the prized pet. "This is yours, little Missy," as he called her. "Meet your new friend."

Katy set the lantern down and stooped to pet the ball of black fur that was attached to Timar's leash. At first, she was a little cautious until Timar handed the rawhide tether to her.

"Oh, Timar, it's just what I wanted. This is the best pet anyone could ever want," cried Katy, as she gathered the kicking, scratching cub into her arms.

Chapter Four
Captured

Amos Boggs took the ferry across the New River, along with his newly aquired horses and supplies. He was proud of himself for putting one over on Captain Wilson. With the added horses and supplies, he would be able to trade for a boatload of fur pelts from the Indians and float them down the James River to Lynchburg, where he could sell them. A boatload of furs would make him a rich man, thanks to the generosity of the British army.

Boggs planned to quit the scouting business, but never seemed to save enough money to get a stake. Now, it seemed, by his underhandedness, he would be able to start a new venture. He was not an educated man by any stretch of the imagination, but he had enough common sense to at least dream of the day when he could settle down and raise his own family. That is, if he could stay away from the taverns, which always managed to get the lion's share of his hard-earned money.

He left Old Jake, the ferryman, standing on the mooring dock and rode off to the east with his newly-acquired horses and provisions. In his pocket, he carried the leavings of his three-months of back pay. Most of it had been gambled away with the British troops in a game of chance, which lasted most of the night.

Trying to rid himself of a hangover, Boggs reached into his saddlebag and produced a bottle of rye whiskey and took a long swig, draining the contents. When the alcohol took effect, Boggs felt better and urged the horses on toward the cave where he'd left his stash of supplies and three horses.

"Won't be long, now," he said to himself as he topped a forest-covered hill a mile from his hidden cavern.

Boggs had been scouting for the best part of twenty years and knew as much about the forest and tracking as any man. He cautiously dismounted, tied the horses and proceeded on foot to check out the cave. Three days ago, he'd left the cave, concealed with underbrush, to report to Fort Chiswell. He wanted to make sure his hiding place had not been discovered or compromised before bringing up the other horses and supplies.

Moving cautiously, it took Boggs more than three hours to cover the short distance between the cave and where he had left the horses. When he finally reached his goal, he found everything outside the cave just as he had left it. Nothing was disturbed and no sign of intruders could be found around the opening of the cavern. He felt satisfied that everything was still safe behind the brush-covered entrance.

Slowly, he pulled back the branches and slipped into the darkness of the cave. He could smell the horse droppings and musky odor of the damp cavern and waited until his eyes became adjusted to the darkness. When he moved toward the rear of the cavern, one of the horses emitted a startled neigh, assuring the hunter that his booty was still intact. Instead of going further, Boggs retreated from the cave, leaving everything the way he found it and returned to get the two horses he'd left behind.

An hour later, Boggs tied his horses to a tree just outside the cavern and began pulling away the brush covering the entrance. Distracted by the stir of the horses inside, he failed to notice the fresh moccasin print in the dirt.

Suddenly, four black-faced Shawnee warriors dropped from the ledge above the cave entrance and were upon Boggs before he could defend himself. Armed with war clubs, they tore into the scout with the fury of madmen, hacking away with the business end of their weapons. He managed to reach the knife on his belt, and tried to fend off the attackers by slashing at them with his hunting knife, but they kicked it away before he could use it.

Boggs had no chance to reach his rifle which he had left hanging on his horse. He cursed himself for being so careless. Now he would pay dearly for that mistake.

Unable to throw the Indians off, he decided to submit to them and take the consequences. He stopped struggling and hoped it would stop the thrashing he was receiving, but they continued to beat him mercilessly. He felt his arms go numb with the blows from their clubs, as his blood spurted upon the faces of his attackers.

It was all over within a matter of minutes. He could see that his chance for survival was quickly disappearing. Boggs felt the darkness close over him as the noise of the shouting Shawnees faded into oblivion.

When consciousness finally returned to the beaten scout, he realized he was not yet dead, even though every muscle and bone in his body ached. He could feel the blood running down his mangled face and tried to move, but realized he was bound with rawhide ropes. He could see through one swollen eye that he was tied across one of his horses.

Boggs could hear the Shawnee warriors squabbling over their good fortune as they went through his belongings. They were dividing the packed supplies between themselves and he knew it was only a matter of time until they discovered the whisky stored in his saddlebags.

"There ain't nothing worse than a bunch of drunk Injuns on the warpath," he said to himself, knowing things were only going to get worse.

A loud whoop from one of the braves told Boggs the whisky had been discovered. His only hope was that there might be enough whisky to make them so intoxicated that he might have an opportunity to escape. He began to think of a way to loosen the ropes, but he was unable to move his hands, which were swollen and bruised. As hard as he tried to move them, his legs and feet were secured so tightly he couldn't feel them.

The squabbling between the Shawnees went on for hours. His captors fought among themselves for the contents of the pack animals, strewing much of it on the ground as their bickering soon became a free-for-all. When they finally divided the supplies, they drew lots for the four horses.

Amos Boggs drifted in and out of consciousness while strapped to the horse. He couldn't feel anything except the dull throb in his head where they clubbed him. Dried blood clung to his face and hindered him from seeing very much through his one good eye, but he could tell by the sounds of the Indians loading his horses that they were getting ready to leave. He only hoped they would leave him behind.

Suddenly, one of the savages grabbed Boggs and threw him off the horse. He hit the ground with a force that caused him to black out again. When he came to his senses, he was stripped naked with his hands tied behind him and his feet were tethered together with leather straps.

The Shawnee who jerked him off the horse, proceeded to fasten a length of rawhide rope around his neck and gave it a hard tug, pulling the injured scout toward one of the horses. He handed the rope to the mounted brave and climbed aboard the remaining horse, leaving Boggs standing bare and bleeding. Then, without a word between them, they struck out through the forest, pulling the white man along behind.

At first, the old scout found the strength to keep pace with the horses, but as the day wore on, walking became unbearable. The rope around his neck tightened when he lagged, causing him to choke, and he would gather the strength to step faster to gain slack in the rope. His feet and legs became running sores as he stumbled over the fallen timber and through the brier thickets. He could feel the gut-wrenching throb of the thorns in his bloody feet as wave after painful wave flooded his throbbing brain. He cursed his captors for not killing him.

The almost never-ending night finally gave way to the morning sun, which began to rise over the forest. The party of savages finally drew to a stop in a forest clearing and made preparations for their morning meal. They tied Boggs to a rough-barked tree and left him sitting naked and alone while they ate their pemican and dried corn.

He was not sure about being thankful that he was still living; nor was he grateful to have made it through the torturous night on the trail. Boggs knew what faced him in the coming days from the stories of those who had been fortunate enough to escape the Shawnees. He wished they had killed him at the cave.

Chapter Five
The Visitors

Josh and Tobahana pulled the loaded travois across the ford and joined Meriah, who anxiously greeted them with a hug for her brother and a kiss for Josh.

"We have visitors," she said, as they lowered their loads. "Three hunters, who have been to Kentuckee and want to talk to you. One is wounded and is unable to travel."

"How long have they been here?" asked Josh.

"They came this morning about sunup. I helped get the wounded one across the creek and into the cabin. He's hurt badly with an arrow wound in his chest," replied Meriah. "I have done all I can for him. If he lives, it will be by the grace of the Great Spirit."

Josh picked up his loaded travois and started toward the cabin, followed by Tobahana and Timar, who were also anxious to meet the recent guests. Meriah and little Katy, her hands full with the bear cub, fell in behind the hunters and followed them to the storage house near the cabin.

Josh laid down his load and told the others to put the meat in the storehouse until morning, when they would have time to process it. Then, he and Meriah went into the cabin to see to the visitors. Tobahana and Timar quickly unloaded the meat and secured it in the building. In a few minutes, they were also inside the cabin, where Josh was talking to one of the travelers.

"My name is Joseph Holden," said the tall stranger in buckskins. "This here is Jim Monay. That one is William Cool," pointing to the unconcious man lying in the bed. "We've shore had a streak of bad luck."

Holden was a little uncomfortable when Timar and Tobahana entered the room and stood against the wall as Josh questioned him. At first, he only stared as if he were unable to continue speaking, until Josh introduced them.

"These men are my brothers-in-law. They will also want to hear what you have to say," said Josh.

Holden tried to smile, but could not bring himself to acknowledge the Indians who had entered the room. Instead, he addressed Josh. "We left Kaintuck four days ago, dodgin' the Shawnees 'til we got to the Clinche River. Onc't across the river, we didn't see any sign of 'em, so we hightailed it east. Poor Will caught a arrer jest after we made it 'cross the river. Looks like he ain't gonna make it home."

"What were you doing in Kentuckee?" asked Josh.

"Wal, it's a long story," said Holden. "Last year, me and Will hooked up with John Findley and four others, who talked us into goin' with 'em. There was Jim Monay, here, John Stewart, and Simon Kenton, a youngster of only sixteen, along with Findley's partner, Dan Boon, who said he'd been down to the Spanish territory called Florida.

I guess we was purty reckless to travel into Kaintuck, but we'd heered of plenty of game and that the Injuns were further to the north. Old Findley said we could bring enough skins back to make us rich, so Will and me went along.

I ain't never seen so much game in one place. Why, you could stand in one spot and count buffalo all day long. And the elk and deer was jist as plentiful. I tell you it was a hunter's paradise," continued Holden, who was now feeling a little more comfortable in the presence of Tobahana and Timar.

"Wal, everything was going 'cordin' to plan, 'til the Shawnees got wind of white men in their country. We planned to spend the winter huntin', but the Shawnees had another plan. They attacked our camp so many times, we couldn't hunt fer protectin' ourselves.

We fought 'em off with our longrifles 'til we run short of shot and powder. Beat 'em back ever time, 'til we couldn't shoot no more. Old Findley said we'd better make a try for the gap in the mountains, but the Shawnee headed us off. Stewart was killed and Findley, Kenton, and Boon was took by the varmits. Will, Monay and me barely escaped with our scalps. We run without stoppin' for three whole days, makin' it to the Clinche, afore Will was wounded. It took us two more days to get here carryin' him."

"Well, you're sure lucky to be here. It's not everyday that a man can escape the Shawnees and still keep his hair," said Josh.

"It ain't been so lucky for old Will, here. He's apt to die afore morning." replied the hunter. "And it shore ain't doin' Findley and Boon and the boy any good to be captured by them stinkin' Shawnee. They've probably already been skinned alive."

Tobahana stepped forward and introduced himself to the traveler. "I am called Tobahana of Senecas, brother of Josh Mosby's wife, enemy of Shawnee." Then, pointing to Timar he said, "Young one is called Timar, brother of Tobahana, brother of Josh Mosby's wife."

Holden seemed uncomfortable, but reached to take Tobahana's handshake. "Name's Joseph Holden from Pennsylvania, and this here's Jim Monay," he said, grasping Tobahana's hand.

"I fight many times with Shawnee. So has my brother-in-law, Josh Mosby. Shawnee very fierce warrior. Will fight anyone who comes on Shawnee land," said Tobahana.

"Only brave men and fools dare to enter Kentuckee," interjected Josh. "This man, Findley, must be one or the other. I've seen many hunters pass by, never to return from Shawnee country."

"I reckon he's brave enough, and so is Boon. They allowed theirselves to get captured so we could escape. We owe our lives to them for the head start they give us," replied Holden.

"What in the world was a sixteen year old boy going on a trip into Shawnee territory?" asked Josh, knowing the trails were hard enough for an experienced woodsman.

"I heered him tell Findley he was runnin' from the law. Said he'd killed a man back east over a girl," replied Holden. "So, Boon took him along to carry supplies. Reckon he's as tough as the rest. Never complained even onc't."

"Well, they're in a heap of trouble. I doubt if the Shawnees will let any of them go. Tobahana and I were once prisoners of the Shawnees and it wasn't a good place to be. We escaped only by the grace of God," said Josh.

"Shawnee make slave of strong white eyes. Maybe they still alive. Maybe get chance to escape, also," said Tobahana, recalling the ordeal he and Josh went through more than ten years ago.

"I hope you're right," replied Holden.

William Cool stirred momentarily, catching the attention of everyone in the room. He coughed and tried to sit up, but was so weak, he fell back in bed. With a voice that was barely audible, he spoke.

"Guess I ain't gonna make it much longer," he gasped. His eyes were beginning to get cloudy as he continued. "Joseph, tell my family what happened. They'll want to know."

Holden lowered his head to hear the last words from William Cool. "Tell them where they can find my grave. They'll want to know......," his voice faded into silence.

As the sun broke into view over the eastern mountains, they buried William Cool on the small hill above the Mosby cabin. He was laid to rest near the graves of Josh's first wife and their two small sons.

Holden and Monay stayed and helped Josh process the meat from the hunt. Each piece was trimmed and layed on shelves in the smokehouse. Josh packed salt, in abundance, over the elk hams and shoulders and hung several strips of tenderloin in the back of the smokehouse where it would be smoke-cured. Tobahana and Timar returned in the late afternoon with another load and assisted in preparing it.

Timar was proud of the black bearskin he'd retrieved from the hunt. He showed it to Meriah and asked her to help him cure it. He wanted to place it in front of the hearth when it was ready. He said it was his gift to the family.

While the menfolk sat on the porch and talked, Meriah prepared the evening meal. She was glad to have fresh meat, even though it was bear rump. Timar insisted that she cook bear meat, since he had taken special pains to retrieve just the right cut from his kill. She finally gave in to his plea and decided to please her little brother.

Meriah cooked a fine meal consisting of the bear rump roast cooked with white potatoes, beans and carrots, seasoned with salt and hot peppers grown on the farm. In a covered skillet, she baked a large cake of corn bread in the hot coals beneath the stew pot and topped the meal off with a wild raspberry cobbler.

The men ate until they couldn't hold anymore. They complimented Meriah each time she refilled their plates. Timar also received some credit for the meal when Tobahana said it was the best way to tackle a bear. Everyone laughed, but Timar didn't think it was so funny. Somehow, he felt he had gotten even with the bear for putting the claw marks on his back.

After supper, the men gathered around the fireplace in the main room of the cabin. Holden offered his tobacco pouch to Josh, who politely refused it and took out his own. Tobahana and Timar did not smoke but enjoyed the smell of the aromatic tobacco as it rose from the clay pipes.

"Guess we'll head t'ward home tomorrow," said Holden. "I shore hate to go without old Will. His folks will be disappointed when he don't show up with me and I hate to be the one to tell 'em the bad news."

Josh spoke again about how dangerous it was to enter Shawnee territory. "A man would have to be a mighty good woodsman to try to winter in Kentuckee. I know of a few who've done it, but they were Cherokees. The Shawnee don't take kindly to anyone taking game from their hunting grounds."

"I'll tell you one thing for shore, that was my last trip to Kaintuck," replied Holden. "When I get back home, I'll find a safer way to make a livin'."

"Life out here on the edge of civilization is hard. Unless you make friends with the Indians, a white man doesn't have a chance," said Josh. "We've been fortunate to have the Cherokees as our friends. They have been good neighbors."

"I've been to Kentuckee with my Cherokee friends," said Timar. "We have hunted there for several summers. We saw Shawnee sign on many occasions, but never got close to any."

Holden was surprised at Timar's excellent command of the English language. "You speak English very well," he said.

"Josh and my sister, Meriah, have been patient enough to teach me the English language. I have lived here with them for over ten years," replied Timar, who went on to ask Holden where he and the others were camping in Kentuckee.

"We planned to make our winter camp at a place the Indians called Licking Creek. There was plenty of salt to cure our meat and fresh water. Old Findley said we'd need to watch out for Shawnee, who would also be needin' salt," replied Holden. "He shore weren't wrong. Them blasted Shawnees tried to run us away from the salt licks ever chanc't they got."

He continued to talk about their plans at Licking Creek. "Young Kenton called our camp Blue Lick, because of the way the morning dew on the grass looked bluish. In fact, about everwhere you looked, the grass seemed to give off a misty blue color. Wal, Findley said we'd found jist the place to do our winter huntin', when he saw the hot steam offen some of the ponds nearby. Said they was hot springs, similar to the ones over in Virginny."

Holden pulled on the clay pipe and continued, "He was right about them springs bein' hot. We all took a bath in 'em. Nearly scalded my skin plumb off, but I got the cleanest bath I'd had for years."

"How far would you say Blue Lick is from here?" asked Josh.

"Wal, I guess it's a good six days, 'less you're runnin' from Injuns," replied Holden. "The three of us run without stoppin' for the first three days."

"Could you draw us a rough map of the trail you took getting to Blue Lick?" Josh asked again.

"Wal, I didn't take notice of any landmarks on the way here, but I guess I know the way from where we started out in

Pennsylvany" replied Holden. "Findley had a map and went over it several times with us. Guess I could recall most of it."

Josh produced a piece of paper from one of the few books he and Meriah owned and handed it to Holden. He called for Meriah to bring quill and ink from the kitchen. On the floor in front of the fireplace, Holden scratched out a crude map, showing the trails the hunting party took to get to Licking Creek.

They began their journey back in April, following the Ohio River along the northern side of the Virginia colony and headed in a southwesterly direction after they reached the falls of the Ohio. Findley was using an old map made by an old trapper who had ventured into Kentuckee many years before. He left the map with his family, who also knew Findley, and let him copy it.

Holden explained how they came to Licking Creek. "We didn't see much Injun activity on the way through the tall grass prairies. Boon said we'd run into some, but they never 'peared 'til we made camp. On the way from the Ohio, we followed a river called the Big Sandy 'til we reached far enough inland to look for a good camp. Reckon we was lucky to miss the Shawnee on our way to Blue Lick."

Tobahana studied Holden's crude map and recognized the spot designated as the Falls of the Ohio. "This where we cross Ohio to see Shawnee chiefs," he said looking at Josh. "Most Shawnee live on north side of river. Only come south to hunt and fight with white settlers."

"The Cherokees talk of a Shawnee called Black Fish, who is a bad character," said Josh. "It wouldn't surprise me if he wasn't the one who caused all the trouble at your camp."

Timar spoke of the stories told by his Cherokee friends. "Sequah and Menah told me about Black Fish. They said he is a fierce warrior who is not afraid of anyone. He is chief of about five hundred warriors who roam the entire territory of Kentuckee, from the great river in the west, to the beginning of the Ohio River."

"Wal, they shore chased us outta the country," said Holden. "I hope old Findley and the others are still alive."

Josh Mosby knew the Shawnees would never let the hunting party escape from them. He had been in their position and was never given an opportunity to sneak away from his captors; although at the time, he was too weak to try it. They kept a rawhide rope around his neck with his arms and legs tethered, so escape was impossible. Their only chance for survival was to be taken to a Shawnee village where they would become slaves or be traded to another tribe.

Josh abhorred the practice of slavery, even though it was common among the landowners in the colonies. His first wife's father had owned several Negro slaves on his Dinwiddie farm back east, but they were never mistreated like the unfortunate captives of the Shawnees. He had first-hand knowledge of strong men being worked and beaten until only starved, skin-covered skeletons remained to face inevitable death by their captors.

He did not want to tell these hunters about his trip north with Tobahana. Instead, he said they would be on the lookout for news of three white men being captured in Kentuckee. If they heard anything, they would send the information east by a passing traveler.

Joseph Holden and Jim Monay bade farewell to the Mosbys before daybreak next morning. Their visit gave Josh and Tobahana much to think about.

Chapter Six
A Cry for Death

    More than a week later, the party of four Shawnees, with their captive, finally reached their destination. Miraculously, Boggs was still breathing. He had endured the long trail without giving up the ghost, but now, he was only a bloody shell of what used to be a strong man. His mind faded in and out of reality, allowing him only small respites of awareness that he was still alive.

    Black Fish's camp was large, spreading over several acres along the Wolf River in the eastern edge of Kentuckee. Several temporary log structures with buffalo hide tops lined the grassy bank of the river. Many smaller hovels, interspersed between the larger ones, filled in the whole area, except for the open area in the center of the settlement. In the middle of the open area stood a large pine post which had been sunk into the hard ground.

    The four Shawnee warriors dragged their prisoner through the village, while many of the inhabitants emerged to gaze upon the poor human at the end of the rope. Several young boys ran out to touch the white prisoner, while others pelted the bloody form with stones. The captors made their way to the post in the center of the village, where they made a game of tying Boggs' frail form to it. When they finally stopped antagonizing their prisoner, they left him hanging on the post with his arms stretched and tied over his head.

    During the long torturous hours before sundown, Amos Boggs became the focal point of harassment by the Shawnees. It seemed as if everyone in the entire village took a turn at beating him, pulling at his red beard and spitting on him. Old women laughed and made obscene gestures as they gazed upon his naked body hanging helplessly upon the pole. Young Shawnee boys ran to count coup by slapping the helpless man on his bloody face, then retreating to chatter amongst themselves.

As the sun lowered toward the western sky, the Shawnees began to tire of their inhumane treatment of the prisoner. One by one, they vacated the town clearing and returned to their living quarters, leaving Boggs alone, barely alive, still stretched upon the post. He no longer felt the wounds he'd received from his captors. Other pains now grew more intense as he tried to relieve the terrible tension caused by his sagging body.

He could barely feel the ground beneath his bloody feet and stretched his toes to raise himself a few inches to allow air into his lungs. When he felt himself passing out, Boggs drew in enough air to sustain him until he could touch the ground again. He knew if he lasted through the night, more punishment awaited him, and if not for the glimmer of hope that came from somewhere deep inside, he would just let death claim his mangled body. Boggs was still alive when darkness enclosed the Wolf River valley.

Sometime during the night, two Shawnee braves cut Boggs from the post and dragged him through the settlement to a fenced compound, where they threw him into a small cage made of pine saplings. He awoke sometime during the night to find that he still lived, although every inch of him ached with cramps and soreness from the beatings he'd received. The early morning chill on his nakedness caused his teeth to chatter until the sun finally crept through the cracks in the cage.

No more than three feet square by four feet in height, the cage was too small for a man to stand or lie down. It had probably been built to hold wild animals, such as bear and cougar, evidenced by the claw marks on the inside walls of the structure. It was much too small for a human being to find a comfortable position to lie or stand.

Boggs tried to move around in the small enclosure, but could not ease the cramps in his numb legs. With much effort, he managed to move into a sitting position with his legs drawn up beneath his chin, and rubbed his aching legs until the feeling came back. The muscles in his body told him that he'd been through the worst week of his life and yet, he would undoubtedly face the Shawnee devils again before the day was over.

The stillness of the morning was broken by the sound of drums reverberating through the crisp morning air, heralding the arrival of a new day. An hour after sunup, the village on Wolf River was alive with activity. Smoke from cooking fires rose from many living quarters and spiraled skyward to fade into the cloudless blue, leaving the whole area permeated with pleasant cooking odors.

From his prison cage, Amos Boggs fought the hunger which had plagued his aching body for several days. He couldn't remember when he had eaten his last meal. During the long trek from his capture near the New River, he was given only a small portion of parched corn, which he carried tightly in his fist and rationed himself to only a few kernels once a day. When the corn was gone, his captors refused to give him more, although they gorged themselves on food from his own supply horses.

Now, as the aroma of cooked food reached his nostrils, he was on the verge of stark-raving madness. His hunger pain had replaced the aching muscle cramps which had kept him from getting any sleep during the night in the cage. The thought of a hot meal was the only thing on his mind at the present time. He knew that if he didn't eat, it was just a matter of time until his weakened body would shut down. At least he would be free of the pain and hunger torturing his naked body. At this point, he would have eaten anything to relieve the ache in his stomach.

Just as he thought the death angel was coming for him, two Shawnee women approached his cage, bringing a gourd of water and a wooden bowl containing a warm mush of ground corn. One of the women produced a sharp knife from the folds of her skirt and moved to the rear of the cage, where she cut the rawhide binding from his wrists. The older woman untied the front of the cage and quickly set the water and mush in front of Amos Boggs, tied the enclosure shut and retreated a few steps to watch the prisoner.

He wasted no time in grabbing up the bowl and sinking his face into the warm tasty mush. In less than a minute, the bowl was empty and licked clean. He washed the mush down with water from the gourd, while the two women sat laughing at the bony resemblance of a human figure in the cage.

Within minutes after wolfing down the bowl of mush, Boggs was racked with a terrible stomach pain. He fought with all his might to keep the food down, but when he could hold it no longer, it spewed forth, splattering through the cage's pine poles. Boggs tried to retain some of the food by holding his hand over his mouth, but a painful gut-wrenching spasm of coughing caused him to lose what he had left in his stomach.

The Shawnee women burst into laughter and finger-pointing at the scene in front of them. They had no pity for the poor wretch in the cage and continued to taunt him by rubbing their fat stomachs and imitating Bogg's inability to keep his food down by coughing and spitting. They finally got their fill of fun and walked away, leaving him still grimacing with a pain in his stomach.

When he regained his composure, Boggs used his dirty fingers to salvage some of the regurgitated food from the pine posts. He felt like he had reached the lowest level of humanity, recalling a passage his mother once read in the Good Book, where it said, "a dog will return to its own vomit." Nevertheless, what little food he could salvage might sustain him until the Shawnees saw fit to feed him again. At least, he still had the gourd of water.

An hour or so later, Boggs watched as several Indians passed by, on their way to join others who were congregating in the clearing in the center of the community. He wondered what was so important that the whole clan was gathering. Then, he saw Black Fish emerge from his quarters and the crowd parted to let him walk through.

Black Fish, chief of the village, strode straight through the crowd and on toward the prisoner's cage. When he reached the enclosure, he spoke to Boggs.

"Why does Red Hair, thief of whites, not like Shawnee

food?" he asked. "Maybe Red Hair want to steal food instead."

Boggs knew the women who had brought the food were responsible for this visit by the chief. He wanted to tell him that the food was good, but he couldn't keep it on his upset stomach. Instead, he remained silent, afraid that what he might say would only get him more torture.

Black Fish waited on an answer from the prisoner for several minutes before speaking again. "When sun reaches highest point in sky, we will show ungrateful Red Hair what is punishment for waste of good Shawnee food."

The Shawnee chief turned and walked away, leaving the old scout to ponder what his next ordeal might be. The sun was less than an hour from its zenith, giving him little time to work on the cramps in his legs. If it was to be more punishment, he hoped that death would take him, knowing that he couldn't stand much more.

Boggs drank from the gourd and washed down the remnants of mush he scraped up from inside his prison cage. The small amount of food seemed to stay down this time, easing the constant ache in his stomach. When the water was gone, he returned to rubbing his legs with his freed hands, and untied the leather thongs that were around his feet. Circulation slowly returned, sending tingling sensations into his lower extremities. After a while, he thought he might be able to stand if he were outside of the cage.

As the sun reached its highest point in the blue sky, two braves came to fetch Boggs. He still couldn't imagine what lay in store, but whatever it was, he knew it wouldn't be pleasant. They opened the cage and motioned for him to come out. He crawled through the opening and tried to raise himself to a standing position, but his weak legs gave way, and Boggs fell face-forward on the hard ground. It took several tries before he was able to stand.

Each of the Shawnee braves took one of his arms to steady him as they walked toward the open area in the center of the village. Boggs tried to walk upright, but due to his cramped condition in the cage, every bone in his body ached, causing him to remain in a stooped position with his head bowed. When he was able to raise his head to see where they were headed, he saw two long lines of Shawnee warriors facing each other in the center of the village. At once, he knew what was coming. His next round of torture was going to be the gauntlet.

During his years as a scout, he had known men who had survived the dreaded gauntlet. It was a terrible test of strength and endurance even for a strong man, and he was in no condition to even walk. Surely, they didn't expect him to run through two lines of club-wielding warriors without giving him time to regain some of his strength. When they reached the end of the two lines of warriors, the two braves released Boggs and took their place in the lines.

In a few minutes, Black Fish made his appearance, dressed in a long white doeskin overshirt, carrying his staff of authority. He was an impressive figure as he strode down the lines of warriors to face the old red-haired scout. When he reached Boggs, he turned to face the large crowd which had gathered around the two long lines.

Black Fish raised his staff into the air and held it there as the drums began a long staccato which lasted several minutes. When the drums stopped, he lowered his arm and faced Boggs.

"Now, Red Hair will see what happens to thief," he said, raising his arm and bringing it down sharply.

Suddenly, at the other end of the lines, another naked figure of a white man appeared as the drums started again. He was much younger than Boggs, and looked as if he, too, had suffered much at the hands of his captors. As the drums reached their loudest pounding, they suddenly stopped.

A strong, burly warrior appeared behind the white man and shoved him into the gauntlet of forty savage Shawnee warriors. A loud roar of shouting from the on-lookers erupted as the naked figure fell head-long into the melee of swinging clubs and sticks. The white prisoner immediately threw his hands over his head to protect himself as the first blows rained down upon him.

He tried to get back on his feet, but the pounding blows prevented him from standing. Instead, he went crawling ahead on all fours while the first warriors in the lines pelted his backside with a barrage of punishing strikes, which brought spurts of blood from his bare skin. Each blow was followed by loud shrieks of pain from the white prisoner, which caused the Shawnees to inflict even more punishment by increasing the intensity of their pelting.

As the unfortunate prisoner scrambled a few feet further amid the thrashing blows, he was able to regain his feet, only to be knocked down by a blood-spattering smash in the face by a brute-like warrior swinging a thick walking cane. The young man fell backward unconscious, as the lines gave way to a frenzy of warriors descending upon him. He was soon hidden among the savage crew of club-wielding Indians.

Boggs turned his head away as the savages began an unrelenting attack upon the helpless figure.

When they finally stopped and moved away from the bloody shape on the dusty ground, Black Fish spoke again, "This white thief took furs from Shawnee land. Now, he pay. If he still lives when morning sun come, I will set free to go tell others not to hunt in Kentuckee."

For several minutes, the piercing black eyes of the Shawnee chieftain stared directly into the face of the old scout. Then, without speaking another word, he turned and walked back through the crowd, leaving Boggs standing in the midst of the throng of Shawnees. When Black Fish entered his quarters, the crowd began to disperse. Soon, only Boggs and the bloody body of the white prisoner were left in the open area in the center of the village.

For a while, Boggs stood without moving, thankful for not having been forced to run the gauntlet. In his weakened condition, his mind wondered in and out of reality as he surveyed the gory work of the savages. He wanted to run from the whole scene, but his feet refused to move.

When he finally regained his composure, Boggs knelt at

the side of the tortured victim. He had never seen a human body with such damage, yet still breathing. The poor man's body was a total mass of bloody wounds from his head to the bottoms of his feet. Blood oozed from lacerations covering every inch of his back, legs and face. The Shawnee had savagely beaten the man within an inch of his life.

Using his hands, Boggs tried to comfort the Englishman by wiping the blood from his eyes and mouth. He tried to pull the unconscious man to a sitting position, but didn't have the strength to lift him. Instead, he cradled his upper body into his lap with all the strength he could muster and held him there until the sun dropped into the western sky.

Sometime after sundown, several Shawnee women came to the two white prisoners with water and food. They also brought a large bowl of water and clean rags to wash the survivor of the gauntlet. It was during the cleansing of the man's wounds that he regained consciousness and began to babble incoherently. After they finished dressing the open sores, one of the women rubbed the wounds with a foul-smelling concoction of herbs and earthy plaster, which covered most of his body. Then, four women, each grabbing an arm and a leg, carried the white prisoner into one of the shelters, leaving Boggs sitting alone in the center of the village.

He ate the bowl of mush and drank the gourd of water, and with much effort, was able to keep it in his stomach. In the cold darkness, Boggs curled into a ball and awaited the coming morning and what lay ahead.

Chapter Seven
Kentuckee

The day after Holden and Monay left, Tobahana and Josh discussed the plight of the hunters who were captured in Kentuckee. Once prisoners of the Shawnee themselves, they understood the seriousness of the dangers that faced the hostages. There would be little chance for the three men to escape, unless they had help. By the time Holden made it back home and sent someone to try to free the hostages, it would probably be too late to save them.

"Since we were planning to leave in a few days, what do you think about a trip to Kentuckee? It would only take us a day or two out of our way. Maybe we could check out the situation and see if we could find a way to free the hunters," said Josh.

He recalled the long, lonely days ten years ago, when he was wounded and thrust into a Shawnee prison camp, without hope of escape, until he befriended the young Seneca prisoner who nursed him back to health. That young warrior was now his brother-in-law, Tobahana, who had risked his life many times to save his white friend.

"It will be very dangerous to get near the Shawnee who keep white prisoners," replied Tobahana. "We would be only two against many. Do not like odds."

"I don't like the odds either, but if we don't try, they will surely be put to death," said Josh. "Maybe we can't get close enough to free them. We'll never know until we go and see."

Tobahana saw the graveness in Josh's face and felt his concern for the three men who had fallen into the hands of the Shawnee. He also knew the risks involved in trying to free them. And there was still the plan to return to Fort Pitt. If they were killed or captured in Kentuckee, his mission to assist the new commandant would also fail. He needed time to ponder the situation.

"Let us think on this problem before we decide. Must

consider many things," said Tobahana.

"I know it will be dangerous. I also know that time is not on the side of the prisoners. Let us decide by tomorrow," said Josh.

Tobahana knew the Shawnees were not going to let them walk into their camp and free the hostages. As a young Seneca, he grew up fighting against their enemies, the Shawnee. Once, as a young brave, he faced one of their most feared warriors, leaving him with a scar that he wore until his death many years later. Scarface had sworn to kill Tobahana and his family; had even taken Meriah as his own prize, only to lose her to his ex-prisoner, Josh Mosby.

Long past the midnight hour, he thought about the poor unfortunate hostages and wondered if they were still alive. They seemed to be experienced hunters, according to Holden. If they used their wits, they could have possibly escaped already, then his and Josh's trip into the vast wilderness of Kentuckee would be for naught. Tobahana pondered the situation, until at last, he dropped off to sleep.

Next morning the little cabin was buzzing with activity. Meriah and Katy were cleaning up in the kitchen following the breakfast meal and Timar was trying to persuade Josh and Tobahana to let him go with them into Kentuckee. Because he had been there once before with his Cherokee friends, he thought they would need his guidance into the vast wilderness. He was not making any progress since Josh and Tobahana had already made up their minds that Timar would be needed at home.

"I know the country," said Timar. "I don't see why you wouldn't want me to show you the way," he pleaded, without a response.

Josh knew the young Seneca even better than his brother. It was going to be hard for Timar to understand the importance of staying here and protecting Meriah and little Katy. One thing he had instilled in Timar during the past ten years was recognizing the priority of protecting the home, no matter what, even if it cost them their lives to keep Meriah and Katy safe. Both had agreed.

Tobahana had been up before daybreak, wandering around the little farm, still thinking about the obstacles they would be facing if they went into Kentuckee. He could hear Josh and Timar discussing the trip as he entered the cabin, knowing Josh was right to persuade Timar to stay and watch over the farm while they were gone, but he also understood that this was an opportunity for his little brother to prove himself as a warrior.

Timar had grown into a fine specimen of a man during the ten years since he had last seen him. The years of hard work on the farm showed in his muscular six-foot frame, and although he dressed and talked like a white man, he was still a Seneca. Because he left the Seneca's as a fourteen-year-old boy, Timar missed the ceremonial Indian passage into manhood. Tobahana understood what the young lad was going through, but now was not the time. There would be other opportunities for Timar.

"Timar will stay and protect Meriah and Katy," said Josh. "He wants to go with us but I convinced him that it was more important to stay.

"It is good," replied Tobahana. He placed a strong hand on Timar's shoulder and looked his young brother in the eyes. "You make wise decision to watch over your sister and niece. They will be safe now."

Timar reluctantly accepted the bidding of his brother. "I will protect them with my life. I have looked forward to being on the trail with my big brother, but I also know one of us is needed here. Josh's experience far outweighs mine. When you return, I will be ready to leave with you, my brother."

Tobahana could see the disapointment in the young man's eyes. "Timar will be welcome to go on trail with me when I return."

Josh spoke to Timar, "Would you draw a map of the trail you and the Cherokees used on your trip into Kentuckee? It might be helpful in helping us get through the mountains west of here."

Timar beamed a wide smile and left the room.

Although Tobahana had not given his verbal acceptance to go with Josh to free the hostages, he was waiting on the porch of the little cabin bright and early the next morning. He was not looking forward to the trip, but since Josh was so adamant about looking into the matter, he felt obligated to go. Maybe it wouldn't take them too far out of the way back to Fort Pitt. Besides, he had never been in Kentuckee and this would be a new territory for him to see.

When they were ready to leave, Meriah, little Katy and Timar gathered on the porch to see them off. Katy hugged her Uncle Toba and gave her father a kiss, along with a small lock of her hair, tied with a bright yellow ribbon, which Josh placed into his breast pocket. Timar shook hands with both and bade them Godspeed. Meriah, with tears in her eyes, hugged and kissed her brother, then turned her attention to her beloved husband.

"You will come back to me, Josh Mosby. I know you will look out for each other and I pray that nothing will keep you from returning. I will miss you, my husband," whispered Meriah as she wrapped her arms around Josh.

"I will think about you every moment until we get back. Please be careful and watch over Katy and Timar. You are stronger than Timar, but let him take my place while I'm gone. He will risk his life to take care of you," said Josh. He gave Meriah a long kiss and turned to Tobahana, who was waiting in the yard.

They stood on the porch and waved to them until they crossed the creek and disappeared into the forest.

Tobahana and Josh were dressed in their forest buckskins and loaded with enough supplies to see them through the next few months. They were armed with longrifles and each carried a flintlock pistol in his belt, along with a Seneca tomahawk and long knife encased in a leather scabbard. Strapped across their shoulders were two full powderhorns and a possibles bag containing firemaking equipment and accouterments for their rifles. Each of them carried a laden backpack containing a change of clothes, extra shot and powder, spare rifle and pistol parts, flints and spare striking steel.

Josh wore a raccoon skin hat, pulled tightly over his locks of blonde hair, and beneath the long coat of buffalo skin, he wore one of Meriah's beautifully decorated vests. On his feet were high-topped winter moccasins, lined with rabbit fur, waterproofed with bear tallow to keep his feet dry during the coming snows. Cradled in his arms was the flintlock rifle with the inverted "V" on the stock, put there by the infamous Scarface when he captured Josh many years ago. He was ready to face the elements and the enemies that awaited them in the months ahead.

Tobahana carried a similar load of equipment, but he refused to wear the heavy buffalo coat offered by the Mosbys. Instead, he wore a long-sleeved buckskin shirt decorated with the Seneca markings. He also rejected Timar's newly made raccoon hat and kept his head free to listen for sounds of the forest. On his feet, he wore knee-length moccasins, similar to Josh's, except for the rabbit lining, which he said was too hot.

After bidding farewell, they struck out in a northwesterly direction, which would take them into the tall mountains rising east of Kentuckee. According to Timar's rough map, there would be several rivers to cross and many steep trails to follow before they reached the territory of Kentuckee. Few white men, if any, had ever entered the wilderness of Kentuckee by this route, and Josh felt priviledged to be discovering new lands known only to the Indians that hunted there.

They covered nearly thirty miles on the first day out. Crossing the Clinche River just below the junction of Josh's own Little River, they traversed the high ground, seeking the gaps in the mountains ahead of them. In a deep valley, they came upon another stream as it wound its way through the mountains of western Virginia. They made camp after crossing the stream and were on the trail before daybreak next morning.

As Josh and Tobahana traveled farther, the mountains seemed to rise higher and higher in the deep forest, dropping off into deep gorges and valleys that dwarfed the streams which flowed through them. They followed several streams until they eventually became fresh water springs at the upper ends of the valleys, leaving them with the arduous task of climbing over the next mountain. The rough terrain, still holding the recent snow, slowed their progress to only fifteen miles on the second day.

Near noon on the third day, as they paused for a meal, Josh said, "It's no wonder that white men have never been into this country. I thought the old Clinche Mountains were hard to climb, but these are the worst I've ever seen."

Tobahana, who never seemed to tire, replied. "Timar's map says mountains will come to end when we travel two, maybe three more days."

That afternoon, they came to a small stream flowing in a northwesterly direction and decided to follow it. The going was slow and hazardous as they followed the stream, climbing boulders, and wading where the banks of the stream were impassable. The mountains rose several hundred feet above the stream bed and blocked out the afternoon sun, causing a muted darkness to fall over the entire river gorge. Huge pine and hemlock trees clinging to the sides of the steep mountain seemed to compete for space between the enormous rock formations which jutted outward and upward along the sides of the gorge. Josh and Tobahana marveled at the scene of the white water river splashing its way through the canyon, on the way to the territory of Kentuckee.

"I wish we could see the area from the peaks above us," remarked Josh as they moved along the river. "A man could see for twenty or thirty miles on a clear day."

"Maybe we will return someday," said Tobahana. He was impressed with the heights of the mountains rising above them. Several times, he stopped and raised his head upward to view the peaks.

Timar's map showed a river winding through a long deep gorge which finally joined another larger stream a day's journey farther to the north. So far, his rough map had been fairly accurate and they had followed it; although it was hard to believe that Timar and his Cherokee hunting partners had actually ventured through these forboding mountains.

Before nightfall, several yards away from the river, they

found a cave large enough to shelter them for the night and unloaded their gear. Josh started a small fire at the rear of the cave and began to prepare the evening meal while Tobahana ventured out into the night to scout the area farther down the river. He returned within an hour to say that they were not alone in the gorge. He found fresh moccasin prints on the other side of the river and followed them downriver to a camp about a mile from their cave.

"Shawnee hunting party. I count ten in camp. Maybe more," said Tobahana. "We not able to get around them tomorrow. Must stay here until they move."

"You're right, of course. We need not get into trouble before we get into Kentuckee," replied Josh as he kicked dirt on the fire to put it out.

They resolved to stay in the cave, out of sight, until it was clear for them to venture on down the gorge. It was possible the Shawnee hunting party knew about the cave, so one of them would have to be on guard at all times. At least, staying in the cave sheltered them from the cold November winds that chilled their bones as it blew through the gorge..

Soon, snow would be falling to cover their mountainous surroundings, leaving them with only one passage into Kentuckee. That route was to follow the river until it reached the Big Sandy River many miles from their cave. The coming snow could trap them in the gorge if they delayed their progress for more than a couple of days. They decided to wait at least one more day to see if the Shawnee moved out of their camp.

During the night, Tobahana slipped into the cold night air and descended to the floor of the gorge, where he carefully crossed the swift river. On the other side of the river, the mountain rose steeply into the darkness of the night. He made his way slowly around several ledges, climbing higher into dense mountain forest, on his way to check on the Shawnee camp. When he reached the crest of the mountain, he crept through the mountain laurel and brier thickets until he thought he was close enough to spot the Shawnee campfire.

Tobahana was nearly out of breath by the time he reached the end of the crest. It had taken him nearly three hours to reach the area directly across the river from where he thought the camp was located. In the darkness, he descended the slope until he came upon a large overhang and crawled gently out to the edge, peering down into the river gorge.

From his perch on the ledge, he could barely make out the glimmer of a single fire across the roaring stream, nearly a thousand feet beneath him. He laid on the ledge and watched the camp until he figured he still had enough darkness left to see him back to the cave on the other side of the gorge.

Just before sunup, Tobahana entered the cave to find Josh sleeping. Deciding not to awaken him, Tobahana sat quietly on one side of the small cavern and listened to the wind blowing past the opening. Sleep soon captured his tired body.

Just after daybreak, Josh was awakened by a noise coming from outside their cave. At first, he thought it was a crow call, but as he listened further, it didn't sound like a crow at all. Somehow, it sounded differently than the crows he'd heard many times back on his farm. He gently touched Tobahana's shoulder to awaken him, but he was already aware of the crow call and put his finger to his lips, motioning to Josh to remain quiet.

Tobahana edged close to the opening of the cave and waited for the crow to sound it's gutteral caw-caw again. From the opening of the cave, he would be better able to locate the position of the crow. Both he and Josh knew the sound was not coming from a bird, but was one of the Shawnee hunters, who needed a lot of practice to perfect his crow call.

Several minutes passed before the *"crow"* called out again. Tobahana's sharp ears picked up the sound which led his eyes to the floor of the gorge directly under their hiding place in the cave. He spotted the hunter, even as the Shawnee brave lowered his hands from his mouth. The brave was kneeling on the rocky bank of the river, looking at something on the stones.

Within minutes, two more Shawnees joined the first brave

and stooped to examine the stones. After looking closely at the spot in question, all three stood erect and began to search other stones in their immediate vicinity. Tobahana watched closely as they stood in one spot, searching the river stones with trained eyes.

Suddenly, one of the braves pointed to another area closer to the swift running river. All three moved slowly to the place in question and stooped once again to examine the stones. After a short time, one of the Shawnees turned and pointed to the small cave opening on the side of the mountain.

Tobahana did not move a muscle to give his position away, but waited until the three braves lowered their heads. Without a sound, he moved backward into the cave and signed to Josh that three Shawnees had discovered their cave. He and Josh retrieved their rifles from the rear of the cave and waited for the three braves to climb the side of the mountain to inspect the opening.

Several minutes passed before they heard the rustle of mountain laurel beneath the mouth of the cave. The three Shawnee braves were getting closer. Tobahana laid down his longrifle and reached for the tomahawk on his belt. Josh followed his example and waited for the first brave to come into view.

With an arrow nocked in his bow, the first brave edged upward, closer to the opening and waited for his companions to join him. Tobahana waited until the second brave arrived. With a sudden move, he and Josh raised to their knees and threw their tomahawks, catching the two Shawnees completely by surprise.

Both tomahawks sunk deeply into the chests of the intruders, killing them instantly. The braves lost their footing and fell, tumbling haphazardly from the side of the mountain. Instantly, Tobahana sprang from the entrance of the cave to pursue the third Shawnee, who was now rapidly descending the steep incline as fast as he could go.

When he reached the bottom, Tobahana saw the brave reach the other side of the river and scramble up the other side. In an instant, Tobahana jumped the boulders in the stream, gaining on his quarry, who was not making any progress up the steep grade. As he neared the Shawnee, he saw him stop and put an arrow in his bow. Tobahana ducked the first arrow and before the brave could nock another, he tackled him. Both Indians rolled off the stream bank and fell into the roaring, swift water.

Tobahana proved to be the stronger and overwhelmed the young Shawnee by holding him beneath the icy water until he submitted. He pulled the brave upon the bank and waited until he caught his breath. While the young Shawnee recovered, Tobahana secured his hands behind his back with a rawhide string and signaled for Josh to join him.

Josh crossed the stream, carrying their rifles and sat down on a boulder near the half-drowned Shawnee.

"What will we do with him?" he asked Tobahana.

"This one will tell us how to find way into Kentuckee," replied Tobahana.

The young Shawnee proved to be quite a catch. After the struggle in the stream, they took him back to their hiding place in the cave, where they questioned him at length. Tobahana had a way of extracting information from his enemies which almost always worked. He used his knife to slowly cut away the buckskin breeches of the young brave, and before long, the Shawnee was telling him anything he wanted to know.

He told Josh and Tobahana that he was part of a large hunting party camped downstream. When asked how many were in the party, at first the young Shawnee said there were only three besides him and the two dead braves. Tobahana pressed his sharp knife to the boy's groin and suddenly got another answer. He then said there were twelve in the party, and began to call out their names.

"What name are you called?" asked Tobahana in the Shawnee tongue.

"I am called Tana-qate, son of Tana-notanan, chief of southern Shawnees. He is called Black Fish by the French and English." replied the young warrior.

"How many days to Kentuckee?" asked Josh, in the Iroquois language, which surprised the boy.

"You are on Shawnee lands called Kentuckee already," replied the captive. "You will not leave this land alive. All white men who come to Kentuckee are dead or slaves to my people."

"Do you know a place called Blue Lick?" asked Tobahana.

"Blue Lick is many days north. It is place where Shawnee make salt in summer. Why do you ask when nothing is there during winter days?" said Tana-qate.

Seeing that the young Shawnee was becoming more talkative, they began to ask him of the white men who were captured a month ago.

"I do not know of white men who still live in Shawnee lands. Maybe my father knows," he replied, hinting that they should take him to his father's winter camp at Wolf River.

"We will see Black Fish soon enough," said Tobahana. "What is on other side of mountain?" asked Tobahana, pointing to the other side of the river.

Hoping for an opportunity to let the other Shawnee learn of his dilemma, Tana-qate told them of the high cliffs and tall mountain range on the other side. He also said there was an old trail which followed the crest of the range, eventually leading to a river called Big Sandy.

Tobahana and Josh recalled Timar's map in which he had marked the Big Sandy River. Whether Tana-qate was telling the whole truth or not, at least he had not lied about the name of the river. They knew this young son of a famous Shawnee chief would try his best to lead them into a trap if they were not careful.

They gagged and tied the youngster to a tree nearby and carried the two dead braves up the incline and dumped their bodies in the rear of the cavern. Tobahana covered the entrance with pine boughs and dead leaves, leaving it almost impossible to discover. After disposing of the bodies, they loosed Tana-qate from the tree and led him across the river, where Josh watched him. Tobahana crossed back over the river, carefully covered signs of the skirmish and rejoined them.

When they climbed to the crest of the mountain range,

the view was breathtaking. They could see for miles and miles in every direction, with mountain after mountain rising into the western horizon. The river in the gorge looked like a small shimmering ribbon as it tumbled along, disappearing a mile or so around the end of the mountain. Across the way, they could visualize where they had spent the night in the small cave on the side of a gigantic island of stone, which rose from the river bed. The entire scene held their attention for several minutes before they located the old trail and began their trek into Kentuckee.

They knew the Shawnee hunting party would soon find the cave and the dead warriors. They had a few hours head start and would need to keep moving if they were to survive. In another encounter with the Shawnees, they might not be so lucky.

Tobahana led them along the crest of the mountain range, following a deer trail that wound through mountain laurel thickets and over ridges with dangerously high rocky ledges. From these heights, they could see many peaks and ridges of other mountains rising one behind the other, far into the northwest. They would not have to cross these ranges, but would follow the river through the passes leading north.

Somewhere in front of them, two day's traveling time away, three hostages were either now dead or being mistreated by the Shawnees. They had yet to devise the plan to help free the white men, but at least they had a Shawnee chief's son, who would be a great bargaining tool if the hostages still lived. The other pressing problem was the war party, which would soon discover their trail and be coming for Tana-qate, who was missing from the hunting area.

Nightfall came with a flurry of new snow falling gently upon the forest. Large flakes floated down through the trees and soon began to stick on the forest floor. This was the break Tobahana and Josh were waiting for; the snow would cover their sign and make it impossible for the Shawnee to trail them. Beneath the cover of a stand of tall hemlocks and laurel, they made camp, hoping their pursuers were doing the same.

Chapter Eight
Tried in the Fire

They finally removed Boggs from the animal cage after several weeks of torturous, sleepless nights to a guarded compound where the living conditions were not much better. He was still unable to find rest on the hard dirt floor. The small enclosure made of ten-foot pine poles buried in the ground was completely bare, except for a pile of hemlock boughs and a small hollowed-out log, which they filled with corn husks and water twice a week.

So far, he had borne the merciless beatings and starvation, although he didn't know where he'd found the strength. He wondered many times why they didn't just put him out of his misery. Boggs suspected they had learned of his illegal activities, such as stealing from the government, but he couldn't make the connection as to why they continued to torture him, until the answer became evident when a Shawnee thief was caught stealing from the winter stores.

They showed no mercy on the poor thief. After receiving days of beatings and mutilation, the Shawnees eventually burned him at the stake in front of the whole village. Boggs was forced to watch the terrible incident while tied to his *pole*. One of Boggs' guards told him that was the punishment for thieves. He shuddered at the thought of being dragged out and burned at the stake.

It happened just as he feared. One morning two braves pulled him out of the compound and dragged his limp body to his pole, where many of the villagers were waiting. He noticed the large pile of wood stacked nearby. The shaman in charge of the event ordered him tied securely to the pole so that he was unable to move his arms and legs. Boggs tried to speak, but couldn't utter a sound.

"This is the day old Boggs will see his Maker." he thought, while old women and children carried arm loads of wood and placed them under his feet.

When the time was right, one of the lesser shamans brought a burning torch from one of the lodges and stood near the recently placed pile of wood. The whole village was now assembled in a wide circle around the naked Boggs, who was silent, but stretched his head toward the heavens, not giving the Shawnee the satisfaction of seeing the tears welling up in his eyes.

Black Fish walked stately through the circle and stood in front of the condemned white prisoner. He carried an ornately decorated staff which he raised into the air.

"This white thief will steal no more," he said and lowered the staff.

The shaman stepped forward and touched the torch to the tinder beneath the pile of wood. Within seconds a blaze errupted, traveling upward through the wood and smoke, surrounding the man shackled to the pole. The outer fringe of the pyre was soon afire with flames creeping closer to the condemned prisoner.

Boggs tried not to cry out. He could feel the heat beginning to touch his bare feet, but could not move them. As the heat grew more intense, large drops of sweat appeared upon his face, erupted and ran off, falling steadily on the smoking pile. When the heat became so intense that he could feel the layers of skin on his feet begin to actually burn, he finally screamed out.

He didn't know how long he'd been back in the compound. When he regained consciousness, the first thing he saw were the blackened, charred feet protruding from his bed of corn husks. They burned so intensely that it felt like they were still in the fire. He had no way to lessen the pain.

Throughout the next few days, he drifted in and out of consciousness, hating the times he was awake which only brought pain and looking forward to the darkness of incomprehension. His feet were running sores, with large blisters, oozing blood and watery excretions. When he looked at them, he doubted he would ever stand on two feet again. He cursed the Shawnee savages who were responsible for his misery, and prayed for death to come and claim his tortured soul.

Three months had now passed since he barely endured the terrible burning at the pole in the center of the town. His feet were almost healed from the burns he received at the stake. He wondered why they pulled his worthless body off the fire and spared his life, but then, he thought of how cruel and insensible the Shawnee were. It seemed to him they were trying to see how much torture a white man could take and still survive. Just when he thought things were getting better, they increased their torture tactics, by starving him for days, then dragging him back to the pole, where more beatings awaited him.

Boggs had lost so much weight that he resembled a skeleton with skin stretched over it. He knew he couldn't survive another trip to the pole. Each time they tortured him, he thought it would be the last time. He couldn't remember when they took part of his scalp, only that he was missing more than half of his hair on the back side of his head.

On one occasion, they cut off one of his ears because he failed to acknowledge what was being said to him. Three of his fingers were hacked off when he reached through a crack in the fence to catch a ground lizard to eat. There were numerous painful burns marks on his body, which had turned into running sores.

Amos Boggs' future was never a question that crossed his mind. He knew he'd never see the outside of this Shawnee village, but there was always hope. Hope that was fading away with each trip to the pole. Still, he failed to give up that small glimmer of hope that eluded him from time to time.

Winter was quickly approaching in the valley of the Wolf River. The compound offered no protection from the elements, and without proper clothing, Boggs was sure to freeze to death. He had heard of the freezing death years ago, when a neighbor and his family froze, and wondered if it was an easy way to go. He was told that a man merely went to sleep, never to awaken. If that were the case, he looked forward to the coming snows.

The November snow storm came and melted and yet Boggs remained alive. The Shawnees finally provided him with a worn out buffalo robe, which he immediately rolled himself into and slept for days. It was the first time he'd been able to get a full night's sleep since being captured.

After that first snow, he began to receive better food, although it was not white man's food. It was mostly scraps, left over from the tables of the Shawnee. Boggs was glad to get their leavings of corn cobs, animal bones and slop. It was never enough to sate his hunger, but he managed to regain some of his strength.

He learned to extract the bone marrow by crushing the bones against the compound fence posts, extracting meager bits of marrow, which provided him with much needed nourishment. The corn cobs he also crushed and ate the centermost part with a sharp stick he'd managed to hide from the guards. The slop, as he called it, was a mixture of scraps from many tables and tasted terrible, but Boggs ate it, thankful for every morsel.

Boggs was still alive when the Shawnee war party returned from their trip to the white hunter's camp on Blue Lick. He watched the three new captives being dragged through the center of the village, amid the savage bystanders who pelted them with stones and clubs. He knew what they were about to face and felt for each of them, especially for the young white boy who was being taunted by several Shawnee braves.

Chapter Nine
A Visitor From the Past

Timar saw the three figures approaching long before they reached the creek crossing below the cabin. When they were closer, he recognized his two Cherokee friends, Sequah and Menah, but didn't know the third person, who seemed to be somewhat slower and more deliberate in his step. From the porch of the cabin, he watched them reach the crossing. His two friends help the stranger across the shallow stream.

At first, he thought the third person was wounded or befallen by an accident, but as they came closer, he recognized who it was and leaped off the porch with a shout and ran to meet them. Menah and Sequah were grinning as they watched Timar quickly cover the ground between them.

When he came to within a few yards, he shouted, "Miskka! Miskka! Is it really you?"

He was glad to see the old Cherokee who had been so close to his family, helping them to survive the terrible struggles with the Shawnee many years ago. He risked his life on several occasions to assist Josh and Tobahana in their escape from the French, securing his own freedom in their flight from New France. Old Miskka was as much a part of the Mosby family as anyone, and his name was honored in the naming of Kathrine Miskka Mosby, the young daughter of Josh and Meriah.

"Old Miskka comes to visit one last time before Great Spirit calls this old Cherokee to the spirit world," said Miskka, grasping the arm of Timar. "Timar is no longer boy. Josh Mosby has been good father to you."

"Yes, I am a grown Seneca warrior," replied Timar. "I am glad to see our Cherokee friend from many moons ago. We did not know if Miskka still lived."

"This old Cherokee has seen more than eighty summers. I wanted to see my good friends one last time. Your two friends have brought me to the home of Josh Mosby. They speak well of you and his family." said Miskka.

"Tobahana and Josh are not here. They have gone into Kentuckee to find three hostages captured by the Shawnee. I am sorry that you will not see them," said Timar.

"I am sorry, also," replied Miskka. "Does your beautiful sister, Meriah still live here?"

"Yes, and she will be happy to see her old friend," Timar said. "She and little Katy are going to be surprised to see you." He took the old man by the arm and led him toward the little cabin.

The toothless, old Cherokee seemed overjoyed at the thought of seeing the beautiful Seneca wife of Josh Mosby again. He had thought of her often, wondering if she ever returned to her people.

"Meriah! Meriah!" shouted Timar as they climbed upon the porch. "We have visitors!"

Meriah opened the door to see Menah and Sequah standing beside Timar. All three had wide grins on their faces. She started to speak but noticed that someone else was also there, standing behind Timar. When the old man stepped forward, she recognized him immediately.

"Miskka! Is it really you?" she said, throwing her arms around the old Cherokee.

"Yes, Princess, it's your old friend," he said, holding her in a tight embrace. "I have traveled many day's journey to see my friends before this old man dies."

"It is good to see our old friend," replied Meriah. "You are still the brave warrior who helped rescue my husband and brother. We have loved you all these many years, thinking you had gone to the spirit world."

Old Miskka released Meriah and stood straight and tall, his head of white hair flowing over his shoulders. A toothless grin broadened his wrinkled face with eyes still bright and clear. "Miskka will soon be with ancestors," he replied. "But first, he will see Josh Mosby and Tobahana before the Great Spirit calls."

"Then you have come to stay with us for a while. I'm sure Timar has already told you that Josh and Tobahana are on the trail again. They will not be coming back until spring," said Meriah.

Old Miskka nodded and said, "There is still much life left in this old Cherokee. He will wait, if Meriah will put up with him through the winter."

"Oh, yes! That would be our pleasure," said Meriah. "You are very welcome to stay for as long as you like. Josh and Tobahana will be overjoyed to see you again."

"Then, it is done," said the old man. "I will not have to return to Cherokee camp with these two young braves."

Meriah invited all into the house where they were welcomed to join her and little Katy at the dinner table. As they took seats, Meriah introduced little Katy to Miskka.

"This is our daughter, Katherine Miskka Mosby," she said. "She is named in honor of the great Cherokee warrior who brought my husband and brother back to the Painted Mountain."

Old Miskka, bursting with joy and pride, reached out to the shy little girl in front of him. She reluctantly submitted and he placed her upon his lap. Everyone around the table was smiling as the old Cherokee looked into Katy's big blue eyes and tried to hold back the tears that appeared in his own.

"You are the daughter of Meriah, princess of the Senecas. You are also the daughter of Josh Mosby, greatest white hunter this old man has ever known. You are named Miskka because that is what I am called. Your mother and father have given you my name because we have traveled many trails together. I am honored to know you, Katherine Miskka Mosby," said the old Cherokee with pride.

Little Katy liked the friendly wrinkled old face at once and extended a finger to wipe the tear that ran down his cheek. "I have a new pet. Want to see?" she said, jumping down from Miskka's lap.

"Not now, Katy. Our guests are hungry and we must feed them first," spoke Meriah.

She excused herself and began setting plates around the kitchen table. Within a few minutes, everyone was enjoying Meriah's good cooking. The old Cherokee expressed his thanks several times as he reached for the large bowl of hot stew to refill his plate.

The next morning, Timar's plan was announced at the breakfast table. He had spent the entire night formulating what he considered to be his greatest adventure. His plan included his best friend, Sequah, who would be his traveling companion. Menah, his other Cherokee friend, having to return to the winter camp, would ask the Cherokee hunters to occasionally check in on the folks at the farm. But most importantly, his plan would also depend on his sister's approval and Miskka's agreement to take his place while he was gone.

"Absolutely not!" was Meriah's response to his plan. "You know what you promised Josh and Tobahana. They expect you to stay here and help us get through the winter."

"But Meriah, you know how much I have wanted to go on the trail. Tobahana himself told me that I was ready. Besides, I'm leaving with him when he returns in the spring, anyway," pleaded Timar.

"Then, you'll just have to wait until they return," replied Meriah.

Timar could see that his plan was quickly being squelched even before he could explain why it was so important to him. He also knew how hard it was to convince Meriah, who stood firmly against his going on the trail. Yet, he wasn't about to give up on an idea that he hoped would make him a full-fledged Seneca warrior.

"But, Meriah, this is my only chance to prove myself. All we will be doing is catching up with Josh and Tobahana and helping them bring the hunters back. Besides, they might need our help," pleaded Timar.

"Little brother, you know Tobahana would not approve of your going into an unknown wilderness. You know how dangerous it is in Shawnee territory. What if you and Sequah are killed or taken by the Shawnees? Tobahana would blame me for letting you go," replied Meriah.

Timar could see that he wasn't going to win the argument with his sister unless he had some help in convincing her. He turned to Sequah, hoping he could show her that Kentuckee was not a place to be feared. After all, they had been there before.

Sequah saw that it was his time to speak. "Timar and Menah have both traveled with me into Shawnee lands. We were careful not to be seen by Shawnee hunting parties. We learned much about the land of Kentuckee and where the Shawnee people live."

"Yes, I know you have been to Kentuckee and I worried every minute while Timar was gone," replied Meriah.

Old Miskka, who was engrossed in the conversation, decided to interject a comment.

"This old man has lived more than eighty summers. I have crossed many rivers from here to the great waters in the north country. Huron, French, and Shawnees I have fought in my lifetime," he cleared his throat and continued. "Many years I was slave of Shawnee and French. My young days were filled working in the Shawnee cornfields, where I stayed hungry because they would not share their harvest with slaves. When my hair began to turn white, they sold me to French, who forced me to work on stone forts until I am too old to lift stones."

The young men around the table listened with awe as the old man continued.

"Fifty summers, this old Cherokee lived with hope to be free once more to roam the forests of his homeland. When few days are left in this old life, Josh Mosby and the great Seneca warrior, Tobahana rescued me from freezing death on slave ship. They help me get back to my people and I will never forget their kindness," he said with tears welling up in his eyes.

"I tell you this because it is true and because most of my life was wasted in slavery. When I was a young brave, my greatest hope was to roam the trails in the vast land of the Shawnee. Kentuckee is a place where great herds of elk and buffalo fill the wide valleys and plains of tall grass; where in one day, a strong hunter can kill enough to feed a whole village through the winter,"

Miskka continued to add one more comment, "If this old Cherokee was twenty years younger, he would want to go with Timar and his friends to see this land of Kentuckee."

"See, Meriah," cried Timar, "even Miskka approves of our trip to find Josh and Tobahana."

Meriah knew that Miskka had only added to her problem of convincing Timar to stay at home. She also knew that Timar would persist until she relented. Josh would be more than upset with her for letting Timar talk her into letting him go. After all, they had disobeyed Josh and Tobahana once before, which had gotten them both into trouble. But that happened many years ago when Timar was just a boy. Now, he was a grown man, who was very capable of taking care of himself.

"If I let you go, who will do your chores and take care of Katy and me?" asked Meriah. "We cannot ask our guest to do your work."

Miskka spoke again. "It is not work for this old man. It would be a pleasure to be useful again. I can still do the work of two young braves. You would bring much honor to me if you let me take the place of Timar until he returns from Kentuckee. I will be here when he comes back to tell me of his adventures."

"Thank you, Miskka!" shouted Timar. "See, Meriah, everything will be alright. Miskka even wants me to go."

"Then you and Miskka will be the ones who answer to Josh and Tobahana. You know it is against my wish, but I cannot stop you from going.

Timar was so excited that he circled the table hugging everyone. When he reached Meriah, he grabbed her in his strong arms and kissed her cheek. "Thank you, my sister. I will be careful and come back with Josh and Tobahana."

Chapter Ten
On To Blue Lick

The three travelers followed the river as it wound its way through the gaps in the mountains, leading them deeper into the territory of Kentuckee. The dense forest was becoming easier to traverse, opening up to snow-covered meadows of tall golden broomsage and green cedars nestled between ranges of Appalachian heights. The stream they were following had long since emptied into a larger stream which coursed its way north.

Timar's map had served its purpose, getting them through the gorges and into Kentuckee, but now they were past the markings on his directions. The land around them was new to Tobahana and Josh. They had no doubt their Shawnee prisoner knew exactly where they were, but they couldn't rely on his guidance for fear that he would lead them directly to the Shawnees.

According to Holden, the place they were looking for was north of where they presently were. He said to look for the blue tinted grass and hot springs nestled in a valley four days running time from the Clinche River. They had been on the trail for over a week, stopping several times along the way, avoiding Shawnee sign, skirmishing with the hunting party where they had taken their prisoner, and keeping their own tracks covered.

The young Shawnee brave had not been very cooperative, either. He tried to escape several times, giving Tobahana a lot of trouble to catch him and bring him back. They tied his arms behind his back and tethered him to Josh's belt where he could keep a constant watch over Tana-qate.

Three mornings after leaving the cave in the gorge, they came upon the valley of smoking springs. In the snow, the plumes rising from the springs drifted upward and dissipated in the cold atmosphere, giving them a strange, scenic view. Around the springs, bluish green grass grew from beneath the snow-covered valley floor. Several elk and whitetail deer munching at the tender grass bolted off as the travelers came into view. Near the edge of the forest, a hundred yards away, they spotted the remains of the white men's camp.

Nothing was left, except for the pine poles they had used to make a shelter. Tobahana scoured the area closely to see if there were any sign. Beneath the snow, several feet from the shelter, he stumbled on the naked, decomposing body of John Stewart.

"We'll give him a proper Christian burial," said Josh as he looked at what was left of the animal-ravaged body of the white hunter.

"Must not stay long," said Tobahana. "Shawnee might come to hunt here."

Tana-qate spoke for the first time in several days. "My family will find me here and kill you. They come to smoking springs to hunt elk in winter."

After burying Stewart, Josh wanted to take a quick bath in the hot springs, but Tobahana convinced him that it would be too dangerous to spend any more time at Blue Lick. With their prisoner, they gathered their packs and moved into the cover of the forest.

It was by accident that Tobahana discovered the mark on a tree. It was scratched into the side of a large poplar tree, no doubt by one of the hunter's belt buckles. The mark resembled a crudely made arrow, pointing south. It was not much to follow, but they decided it was put there to show which direction the hunters were being taken.

"We must be very careful," said Tobahana. "Shawnee might know about tree sign."

They left the lower forest and climbed into the higher elevations of the mountains, still traveling in a southerly direction. That night they made a cold camp beneath an overhanging cliff, several miles from Blue Lick. After they had eaten and secured the prisoner, Tobahana left for a night of scouting the area toward the south.

Before daybreak, he came back to tell Josh that he'd spotted the main camp of the Shawnees. It was a large village along the banks of a small river within two hours of their present camp. He said there were many lodges but saw no movement about them.

"Now, we must make plan," said Tobahana.

Before the morning meal, Josh and Tobahana formulated a plan to determine whether the hostages were at the Shawnee village. Since the Shawnees were on the warpath against the whites, Tobahana suggested that Josh remain here in camp with their prisoner until he scouted the village more closely. If he were discovered, he would receive bitter treatment if captured.

Their plan called for a meeting with the chief of the village to inquire about the captured white hunters. Knowing they had an edge, having a hostage of their own, they felt that the Shawnees would be willing to agree to a trade. That is, if Tobahana could get to the chief without being killed.

"You guard Tana-qate close. He will try to escape with only one to keep watch," said Tobahana. "I will be back when moon rises. If I do not come back, take prisoner back to Blue Lick. Will meet you in two moons."

Before leaving, he checked the bindings of the prisoner and removed the necklace from Tana-qate's neck. "This will tell Shawnee chief we have son," said Tobahana, stuffing the necklace into his shirt.

He bid farewell to Josh Mosby and disappeared from view, entering the evergreen forest below the overhang. There was no doubt about the danger of approaching the Shawnee village. There would be sentries posted and hunting parties coming and going during the daylight hours.

Tobahana decided to enter the village at the main entrance. There was no use sneaking about, trying to find the prisoners. If they were there, he would probably be caught and then the circumstances would be worse. At least, by approaching the village straight on, he would be considered a visitor instead of an intruder, even though he would most likely be unwelcome.

From the rise, he could see the main entrance and made

his way toward the Shawnee village. As he approached, several young braves were having target practice in a clearing near the path leading to the main part of the village. He walked steadily toward his goal with several of the braves falling in behind him. Most likely, they had never seen a Seneca warrior and were intrigued at this stranger who seemed to pay no attention to them.

Tobahana was most certainly a formidable figure. Dressed in his Seneca clothing, a longrifle cradled in his arms, tomahawk and longknife in his belt, he looked every inch a warrior who was not to be taken lightly. Two eagle feathers, signifying warrior status in the majority of the Iroquois tribes, graced the back of Tobahana's head. He was much taller and broader than the young braves who walked behind him, keeping pace, but not too closely. As they passed the first few lodges, several other braves joined in and followed along, curiously interested in this new visitor who seemed to know where he was headed.

Tobahana had been in Shawnee villages before. He knew the basic layout of their encampments and where the chief's lodge usually stood. When he reached the center of the village, he stopped in the clearing at the blackened pine post and waited.

It didn't take long for news of a visitor to reach the ear of Black Fish, who was meeting with his lieutenants concerning the new prisoners. One of the young braves entered the lodge and interrupted the meeting by whispering in Black Fish's ear. Silently, he rose from the seated council and followed the young brave outside.

Black Fish, wrapped in a long buffalo robe, strode toward the tall Indian standing near the prisoner's post. A few feet from Tobahana, he stopped and folded his arms as if waiting for the visitor to speak first. He wore the familiar Shawnee shaved head, except for a tuft of black hair, which radiated from the back like a black sunray. There was no warpaint to enhance the black, piercing eyes that stared directly into the eyes of the intruder.

They stood silently for several minutes until Black Fish finally spoke in the Iroquois language.

"Why has this foolish Seneca come to the village of the

great Shawnee Chief Black Fish?" he asked.

Tobahana didn't like the word "foolish" in Black Fish's question. "I am Tobahana, son of Meniah, former leader of the Ontario Senecas. I have traveled many moons to speak to the great Black Fish, war chief of the Shawnee."

Black Fish studied the impressive figure standing in front of him. He didn't let on, but suspected the timing of the Seneca's visit had something to do with the recently captured whites and waited for him to state his business.

It was not frequent that an Indian spoke for a white eye, but these hostages were different than other captives taken in recent years; they had trespassed on Shawnee lands to hunt game instead of building cabins to raise families. Black Fish, a hunter himself, identified with their desire to take skins and pelts from Shawnee hunting grounds, but also knew if they were allowed to do so, it would only open the territory to more white hunters. So, he decided to teach them a lesson by holding them. If they cooperated, he would eventually let them go. If not, torture and starvation awaited them.

"Why do you visit Shawnee?" repeated Black Fish, becoming impatient with Tobahana.

"I come in search of white hunters," he said, getting straight to the point of his visit.

"Why does Seneca have interest in white dogs who encroach on Shawnee hunting grounds?" asked Black Fish. He could see that this Seneca warrior showed no fear of walking into the camp of tribal enemies.

"Tobahana has been long time friend of white eyes. I work many years for commandant of Fort Pitt to keep peace between Shawnee and English. Now, I hear of white hunters captured at Blue Lick. I am here to take white hunters back," he said, matter of factly.

Black Fish was surprised at the straight-forwardness of Tobahana and wondered how he knew so quickly about the new hostages. It had been less than two weeks since the hunters were captured. He wanted to ask Tobahana, but refrained because he didn't want to admit there were any white prisoners in the camp.

Tobahana stood, waiting for a response from Black Fish. He realized the present danger of being taken himself, but doubted if the Shawnees were interested in another captive in the dead of winter. They would have to expend more of their food stocks to keep him through the months ahead.

He knew they could kill him at any time, thus eliminating the problem of this strange visitor. He had the chief's son, but he wasn't ready to volunteer that information until he knew for certain the hostages were there and whether he could trade Tanaqate for them. He knew he held the key to the white hunters' freedom, if Black Fish was interested in trading them for his son.

Instead of further conversation, Black Fish raised his arm and the circle of armed Shawnee closed to engulf Tobahana. They immediately disarmed him, taking his rifle and hand weapons. Before he could speak, the chief turned and walked back to his lodge, leaving Tobahana at the mercy of the warriors who now held him.

Stripped of his arms, Tobahana could do nothing but submit to their rough treatment. After an hour of humiliating taunting and beatings from the crowd surrounding him, his arms were bound and he was led to the torture post, where they stretched him, arms extended over his head. There, he received more flailings by the women and young boys who ran by, counting coup with their laughter and heckling.

Tobahana had survived the initial confrontation with the Shawnees and expected to receive more beatings at the post before he could get the information he wanted. He was willing to take the punishment, but not looking forward to it. The Shawnee were known for their vile treatment of prisoners, according to the few who had been fortunate enough to escape. He, himself, had experienced survival in one of their prisons more than ten years ago.

This time, he had let himself be caught to gain entrance into their compound here in the Wolf River settlement. He knew if the white hostages were still alive, he would find them in the compound; that is, if he lived through their beatings and was taken there. He hoped that would be the case.

The Shawnee left their new prisoner tied to the post during the remainder of the day. The temperature hovered just above freezing and it looked as if snow was in the night's forecast. Tobahana was already beginning to shiver as dusk enveloped the settlement.

Chapter Eleven
Tana-qate

When Tobahana did not return at the close of the first day, Josh was concerned that the worst had befallen him. He knew his Seneca brother-in-law must have a good reason for not coming back as they had planned. He also knew that Tobahana had been in tough situations before and had always managed to take care of himself. Then he remembered that Tobahana said, if he didn't return today, he would see them back at Blue Lick.

As new snow began falling at nightfall in their camping place beneath the mountain ledge, Josh gathered dry wood from under the ledge and risked building a small fire to cook a hot meal, counting on the snow to conceal the smoke. He produced two pewter cups from his pack, filled them half way with water and added a few chunks of dried deer meat and a handfull of dried vegetables. When the fire was hot enough, he placed both cups at the edge of the glowing embers.

Josh turned his attention to his hostage and asked him if he were hungry. He received no answer but knew Tana-qate hadn't eaten since his capture nearly four days ago, when they had taken him at the cave. He had refused to accept food from his captors, who offered it several times, only drinking water from the streams they crossed.

As the food in the cups began to heat up, a pleasant aroma permeated the area under the overhang. Josh could see that Tana-qate was becoming aroused. Josh knew the young Shawnee was hungry enough to eat both cups of the quick stew but he was hungry himself, not having eaten since the night before. When the stew began to boil in the cups, Tana-qate finally ended his spell of silence.

"Tana-qate would eat with white man if he will share meal," he said, bringing a smile from Josh Mosby.

He untied the young Indian's hands and retied them in

front so he could hold the steaming cup of stew. Josh was careful not to remain close to Tana-qate after he handed him the hot food. He was not comfortable with the situation and didn't want the hot liquid thrown into his face. He took a seat on the other side of the fire and began to sip from his cup.

Josh never took his eyes from his prisoner. While he ate, he watched Tana-qate empty his cup and toss it across the fire where it landed near him. The young Shawnee acknowledged his appreciation of the food by showing his first smile since his capture. The gesture was welcomed by Josh, who asked him if he wanted another cup of stew. Tana-qate declined the offer and resumed his place under the overhang. There, he was again tied with his hands behind his back and covered with a woolen blanket which Josh produced from Tobahana's pack.

"You rest and get some sleep, now. We will be leaving when it gets dark," said Josh.

He didn't know if he could find his way back to Blue Lick at night in the driving snow. But it was a good time to travel with the snow covering their tracks. The best chance for not being discovered was making sure that they left no tracks for a Shawnee hunting party to find.

Josh's biggest problem was Tana-qate. He knew the young brave would try to escape at the earliest opportunity. Another problem was the extra pack of Tobahana's. It was too heavy for him to carry both packs and keep Tana-qate in custody at the same time. He thought about the situation for some time while the prisoner slept on the other side of the fire. Then, he decided on the only solution he could come up with.

"Time to go," he said as he roused the sleeping brave. "You will carry Tobahana's pack."

"Tana-qate not help white eye. I am Shawnee warrior who does not do woman's work," said the prisoner.

"You will do as I say," replied Josh, kicking the blanket off the young man.

He drew the long knife from his belt and cut the bindings from Tana-qate's wrists. He produced a long rawhide rope from his coat pocket, tied it firmly around Tana-qate's neck and jerked him to his feet. Josh wrapped the loose end of the rope around his own waist and tied it securely. Then, he picked up Tobahana's pack and thrust it into the arms of the young Shawnee who immediately threw the pack into the embers of the fire, sending a shower of sparks flying.

Josh gave a sharp yank on the rawhide rope. Tana-qate went sprawling headlong on top of the pack. Immediately the young brave jumped to his feet and faced his captor with drawn fists. He moved toward Josh, bursting loose with a roundhouse swing of his right arm, which caught Josh square on the side of his head and sent him tumbling backward. Tana-qate was upon his captor in a flash, flailing with both fists.

Taken by surprise, Josh tried to cover his face from the blows by the young Shawnee. Blood spurted from his nose and he felt the pounding of fists on both sides of his head. He grabbed the arms of Tana-qate and held on as they rolled on the hard surface under the overhang. He finally regained control of the prisoner by rolling on top of him and subduing his arms.

It was over in a matter of seconds, but Josh Mosby had learned a lesson. He would never take his eyes off his prisoner again. When he regained his senses, he retied Tana-qate's arms behind him.

After applying fresh snow to his nose to quell the bleeding, he washed his face and checked the supply packs. When he was sure that everything had been picked up and repacked, he faced Tana-qate, who was sitting against the back of the overhang with a broad smile on his face.

"You will be glad to carry this pack," said Josh, pointing to Tobahana's pack lying on the ground. "If you refuse, you will not see the sunrise. I will not say it again."

He jerked on the rawhide rope and brought Tana-qate to his feet and told him to turn around. When he reluctantly complied, Josh threw the straps of the pack across Tana-qate's head and secured it on his back with leather thongs. After he checked to see if it would stay on the young Indian's back, he motioned for him to start walking, holding the rawhide rope attached to his neck. Josh picked up his rifle and followed him into the darkness.

The snow continued to fall, dropping large flakes into the already white forest. Although Josh welcomed the snow, it made traveling virtually impossible. He could see only a few feet ahead of them as they made their way through the deepening white that surrounded them. He pushed the young prisoner onward, keeping a taunt hold on the tether.

The way back to Blue Lick was northward, nearly ten miles from the spot where they had last seen Tobahana. They had several mountain crests and valleys to cross and Josh hoped he could find the way in the darkness and blinding snow. He had a good sense for direction, but the falling snow presented him with a vertigo-like feeling as they trudged onward through the forest.

From time to time, he pulled Tana-qate to a stop, so he could check his bearings. He knew he couldn't count on his prisoner to help guide him, but when they came to a small stream in the first valley, he was sure that Tana-qate knew where they were. As they crossed the stream, the young Shawnee seemed to know where to find the right stepping stones.

Through most of the night, the two stumbled along toward Blue Lick. Sometimes, they encountered drifting snow and had to detour from their intended route, but Josh was satisfied that he was on track. Near dawn, the pair of travelers came upon the hot springs, where plumes of steam rose to melt the falling flakes of snow.

Josh located the ruins of the hunting party camp and with the help of Tana-qate, they used the cut logs to improvise a shelter in a near-by grove of trees. When he was satisfied with their effort, he and Tana-qate climbed under the shelter to await the return of Tobahana.

Sometime during the night, Josh was awakened by the wind blowing hard against their shelter beneath the hemlock boughs, sending sprays of snow down upon him. He rolled over to check on his prisoner, who had been tethered to him lest he try to escape. To his surprise, when he pulled on the rawhide rope, he discovered that Tana-qate was gone.

Josh immediately jumped up, knocking a small avalanche of snow down through the boughs, bringing him wide awake. How could he have been so foolish to let the boy escape? Trusting Tana-qate not to try anything had been a terrible mistake. Most likely, the boy was now headed directly to the Shawnee camp.

It was too late to catch Tana-qate since he couldn't tell how long he'd been gone. The driving snow had most likely already covered his tracks, making it impossible to trail him. There was no use trying to recover the prisoner until daylight, knowing the young Shawnee was familiar with the landscape and could probably find his way without much effort in the snow storm.

If Tana-qate reached the Shawnee village by morning, Josh felt sure that their mission would be a total loss. When the boy told Black Fish the news about the two men coming to rescue the hunting party, he would surely send a war party to Blue Lick. And what would be the fate of Tobahana? His mistake would surely cost Tobahana his life.

There was nothing he could do at this moment but wait to see if he could pick up Tana-qate's trail. He knew that the main camp was about twenty miles from his present position, and taking into consideration Tana-qate's agility and knowledge of the territory, Josh figured the young Shawnee would be halfway home by daybreak. He felt helpless to do anything but seek another hiding place and wait to see if Tobahana would somehow return.

Picking up his equipment, Josh crept from the shelter and stood in the falling snow. In the darkness, he knew it was impossible to find any of Tana-qate's tracks, so leaving the shelter, he slowly groped his way deeper into the mountainside, slipping and sliding as he climbed higher and higher. Near the top of the first peak, he found another shelter beneath a rocky outcropping. Here, he dropped his packs and sat to rest, thinking that this was as good a place as any to wait.

    If not for the falling snow, he felt that from this position, he could still see the camping area at Blue Lick. He cleaned out a place under the overhang and made himself a bed of dry leaves which had blown in during the previous autumn. Satisfied that he was safely concealed, he wrapped himself in his long buffalo robe and lay there, listening to the soft snow falling on the tree branches around him. He hoped the snow continued until his tracks were covered.

Chapter Twelve
Shawnee Justice

On the third morning after their imprisonment in the Shawnee village, the hunters were surprised with a visit by none other than the chief. Black Fish, followed by a shaman and two armed warriors, walked into the room and stood facing the three prisoners for several minutes before he spoke.

"I am Black Fish, chief of the Shawnees. White eyes now belong to people of this village. I will decide if trespassers on Shawnee land live or die." He seemed to relish the thought of having the lives of the three white hunters under his control.

Black Fish, wearing his long buffalo robe, stood with arms folded and stared at each of the white men with his piercing black eyes. He expected to see signs of fear, but these men seemed to show none. After he looked directly into the eyes of each, he grunted to himself and pointed to young Kenton.

"When the sun reaches highest point, this one will say if all three live or die," he spoke.

Then, he turned and walked out of the temporary prison. The others followed with wide grins on their faces. They knew what was in store for the younger of the three hunters.

Shortly before midday, two armed braves came to get them. Boon and Finley were taken first, leaving young Kenton alone to face the unexpected event which was to follow. Before leaving, Boon spoke encouragement to the boy.

"Be brave, son. Don't show any fear if ye can help it. 'Twill only make it harder on ye."

It was ironic that after all they had been through during the past few days, it now depended on the braveness of the youngest member of their party. Young Kenton, a large lad for his sixteen years, had proven himself to be worthy of their trust during his time on the trail with the hunters. He'd carried more than his share of the load without complaining, even when some of the others griped about their heavy packs.

John Finley had visited the Shawnees a few years earlier in '67, having been welcomed and treated well by them. His hunting party had no problems with the Indians on that occasion and were allowed to hunt and trade freely. He was puzzled at the resentment of these Shawnees, who seemed to have changed their minds about getting along with the whites.

Finley and Boon understood what was going to occur when they were brought to the center of the village. The whole population of the village seemed to be gathering in the clearing. Two long lines of warriors, armed with clubs and keen willow branches, faced each other in the center of the crowd of milling Shawnees.

At one end of the gauntlet lines, stood an older white man, who tried to cover his nakedness with the remnant of a tattered buffalo robe. His shabby head of red hair and beard above his skeleton-like body set him apart from the Indians.

Somewhere in the village, a steady drum-beat could be heard above the incessant chatter of the villagers. Just before the sun reached its zenith, two warriors made their way through the crowd, pushing young Kenton in front of them. He had been stripped of all clothing, including his boots. The embarrassed boy tried to cover his nakedness by holding his hands over his privates, but the shoving of the two braves made him use his arms to retain his balance. They stopped when they reached the head of the two lines and stood, holding Kenton by his arms.

When the drumming finally stopped, Black Fish made his way throught the crowd and faced Boon and Finley.

"You will now see punishment for trespass on Shawnee hunting grounds. If this English dog still lives when he reaches Red Hair." he said, pointing to the wretched man at the other end of the gauntlet, "you will not die today. If he does not, one of you will take his place."

Black Fish raised his arms high into the air and brought the milling Indians to attention. Quietness returned to the settlement with all eyes upon the event that was about to happen. The warriors in the lines made defiant gestures with their clubs toward the young man who stood at the head of the line. The signal for the gauntlet to begin came when Black Fish lowered his arms.

    Boon and Finley watched helplessly as the two braves holding young Kenton shoved him forward into the melee of swinging clubs. His first reaction was to raise his arms to protect his head from the many blows raining down upon him. He pushed forward, warding off blow after blow to his face and head, while receiving a hammering of clubs to his back and legs. The willow branches cut long, blood-spurting wounds across his shoulders and buttocks, as the Shawnees increased their frenzied beating.

    One strong brave landed a punishing blow to the back of his head, which brought him to his knees. Kenton knew he had to get up and continue through the lines. To stop now meant that the pounding would increase to a point where he would loose consciousness. He winced at the cutting switches which lacerated his back and legs and tried to regain his feet.

    Finley and Boon shouted at the same time for him to get up. They knew if young Kenton didn't get to his feet and make a rush for the other end of the gauntlet, he would die from the punishment he was receiving.

    "Get up, Simon. Make a break for yon end!" they both yelled.

    Simon could not hear over the loud screeches of the Indian bystanders. All he could do was drop to all fours and try to crawl forward against the tide of angry Shawnees. Blow after blow pelted his back and head, as he inched slowly along. Somewhere deep inside, he managed to muster enough strength to come to his feet.

    Up ahead, a tall brute of a warrior stepped out of line and directly into his pathway. He could see the large club being wielded by the big man and feared that the end was near. He knew he didn't have enough strength left to survive the warrior's heavy club.

    It was then that he vowed to go down fighting. With

every ounce of strength he could summon from his bleeding body, Simon Kenton made a daring headlong dash straight for the waiting warrior. At the last second, young Kenton lowered his head and drove directly into the big warrior's stomach, catching him off guard and sending him falling backward.

He leaped over the falling Shawnee and rushed onward through the lines of club-swinging Indians. Several of the bystanders began to shout encouragement to the young white boy as he struggled to reach the end of the gauntlet. He covered his bleeding face again and fought off the steady rain of clubs and switches on his brused and lacerated body.

At last, he reached the end of the gauntlet and fell at the feet of the red-haired white man. He had survived the gauntlet.

Black Fish raised his arms again and the crowd dispersed. The warriors in the gauntlet came to stand around the young white prisoner to observe the damage they had inflicted. As if to say they admired his bravery, one-by-one they grunted their approval as they touched the bleeding youngster.

Black Fish spoke, "This boy will live. He has done what most white men cannot."

Chapter Thirteen
Timar's First Encounter

Before sundown on their second day, the two young braves picked up the trail they had been trying to locate. It was a hard trail to follow. The men who left the sparse indications were good at covering their tracks. Many hours were wasted on false trails, which frustrated the two young trackers as they made slow progress along the river gorge.

They had been here before, but this time, they were on a mission instead of a hunting trip. They had to find two men in a vast wilderness that stretched from their home to the great Ohio River, two hundred miles to the north. Both of them knew approximately where they were, but any deviation from the trail they were following could take them many miles, or even days out of their way.

Halfway through the gorge, Timar looked up to see the small cavern nearly a hundred feet above the river. He motioned for Sequah to watch while he traversed the steep incline to inspect the cave. In a few minutes, he reached the opening and disappeared inside. Several minutes passed before he exited the cave and called to Sequah.

"They have been here," he called. "There are two dead Shawnees inside."

Quickly, Sequah climbed to the cavern and followed Timar back into the darkness. When their eyes became adjusted, they looked over the two bodies, discovering how they had died. Both Shawnees had tomahawk wounds which had taken their lives.

"Not much doubt who killed them," said Timar. "I've seen Tobahana's work before. He and Josh have been here, I'm certain."

Two days later, Timar and Sequah found the camp at Blue Lick. They had made good time since leaving the cave with the dead Shawnee. They were surprised that no one was there. Finding the freshly dug grave presented them with a puzzle, but when Timar recalled the story from Holden, he figured it was John Stewart who was buried there.

The next few hours were spent trying to pick up the trail. After circling the camp several times, they decided to move into the forest to see if they might have better luck. When they located the arrow symbol on the tree, they both knew which direction Josh and Tobahana were heading. Timar knew Tobahana would never leave such an obvious trail marker and surmised that the hunters who had been taken hostage had left it.

The new snowfall soon gave them something else to think about. If there were any signs to be found, they would soon be covered, leaving them only the direction arrow as an indicator. They decided to take a chance and scout the area to the south. Before dark, they found an acceptable camping spot near a small mountain stream. Shedding their packs, Timar and Sequah wasted no time concealing themselves beneath the hemlocks trees near the stream. They decided to wait until morning to resume their hunt for Tobahana and Josh.

Near midnight, both were aroused by the noise of a branch being broken somewhere near the stream, which brought them fully awake. It was not the sound an animal would make; most animals would be bedded down on a night like this. It sounded like a heavy, sharp snap that was most likely human-made.

Timar motioned for Sequah to remain as he eased out of the shelter and into the falling snow. After his eyes became adjusted to the darkness, he carefully moved to where he thought the sound came from. He crept slowly forward until he came to the stream, looking carefully along the ground for any sign. At the edge of the stream, he saw what had caused the noise. A broken branch and a set of footprints were plainly visible in the snow.

Quickly, Timar returned to get Sequah and brought him to see the tracks. There was only one set, made by someone who was in a hurry, otherwise he would not have stepped on a rotten branch. The tracks led southward, along the stream bank, as if the person was looking for a place to cross.

Timar and Sequah decided to follow the mysterious traveler and quickly retrieved their packs from the shelter. Within a few minutes of tracking, the trail left the stream and began to traverse a steep ridge. The track-maker seemed to know just where he was going, leaving the easier way to cross the high ridge.

Timar suddenly stopped and spoke quietly to Sequah. "This man we're trailing knows where he is headed. We will never catch up to him if we don't split up. You follow the stream and I'll go with the tracks. I'll meet you when I get across the ridge and find the stream again."

"Be careful," said Sequah. "I'll be waiting for you."

Timar resumed the trail up the ridge, following the tracks in the falling snow. The going was treacherously slick on the steep side of the incline, and he held onto tree limbs to keep from sliding backward. He didn't know which way the tracks would go or what he might encounter when he reached the top, so he kept his rifle hand free in case.

As he reached the crest of the ridge and started down the other side, he noticed that the tracks made a sudden detour around an outcropping of cliffs. Timar slowed his pace and took time to survey the area in front of him. Beyond the outcrop, the tracks were not visible. They seemed to have stopped.

Timar inched himself closer to the edge of the outcrop of cliffs, noticing that the tracks disappeared just below where he was standing. His first thought was that the track-maker knew he was being followed and picked this place to make his stand. As he waited, listening for any sound coming from below, Timar wished that Sequah were with him. The two of them would have a greater chance to subdue whoever was hiding beneath the outcrop.

After waiting for several minutes, he thought he could hear movement coming from just below. A rustling of leaves confirmed his thinking. The person being tracked was either unaware of being tracked or sure that he was safe.

Timar slowly eased himself around the outcropping to discover that the tracks led underneath the overhanging rock and into a small cavern. At the rear of the cavern, he could see the shape of his quary trying to cover himself in a bed of dry leaves. As quickly as he could, Timar jumped into the entrance of the cavern with his rifle pointing directly at the stranger in the bed of leaves.

"You, there!' he called out, "Come out where I can see you."

The figure in the bed grunted something Timar couldn't understand and crawled forward. When he drew closer to Timar, he stood and faced the one who confronted him. He could see the longrifle still pointed to his midsection and decided not to resist.

"Who are you? asked Timar in the Iroquoian tongue.

The stranger remained silent until Timar punched him in the stomach with the rifle barrel. "My name is Tana-qate, son of Black Fish, chief of the Wolf River Shawnee, and you have made a grave mistake."

Timar replied, "I am called Timar of the Seneca, brother of Tobahana, great warrior of the Seneca nation. You are now my prisoner until I know why you have come to this place."

Tana-qate suddenly knocked the rifle aside and sped past Timar, slamming him with a hard blow to his head. He dived out of the cavern, rolling headlong down the snow-covered incline, careening off trees and bushes until he came to a stop at the stream bed. When he regained his senses, he was looking directly into the barrel of another longrifle.

A minute later, Timar joined Sequah with his prisoner. "Looks like you have recaptured this young Shawnee who calls himself the son of a chief."

"It was no trouble. He just sat there and waited on me to catch him," laughed Sequah.

They tied Tana-qate's hands and led him back up the ridge to the cavern. Inside, they unloaded their packs and began questioning the prisoner.

"Where have you come from on a night like this? Why are you unarmed? Who do you run away from?" were the questions.

Tana-qate remained silent.

"Why is the son of a Shawnee chief alone in the forest?" Timar asked.

When he got no response, he said, "I think this one is a teller-of-tales. He does not look like a Shawnee chief's son. A chief's son would never let himself be taken prisoner."

Sequah realized what Timar was trying to do with his questioning. He also began to ask the young Shawnee what he was doing out alone in this kind of weather.

"Weather is bad for travel after dark. Why does Shawnee risk life for no good reason by traveling alone? You are very foolish boy," taunted Sequah.

"I am Tana-qate, son of Black Fish, chief of Wolf River Shawnees," blurted the youngster. "I will say no more."

Timar and Sequah were both aware that Black Fish was one of the Shawnee chiefs. In fact, according to the hunter, Holden, Black Fish was responsible for the fight at Blue Lick when the three hostages were captured. If what this Shawnee said was true, they were looking at a very valuable hostage. They had only one major problem... where were Tobahana and Josh?

They decided to hold the prisoner until they had time to discuss their situation. One of them would stay awake and guard Tana-qate while the other tried to get some sleep. Timar took the first watch while Sequah made a bed at the rear of the cave and was soon asleep.

Timar kept a sharp eye on the young Shawnee as the night wore on toward dawn. As he sat studying the young Shawnee, he supposed Tana-qate was probably telling the truth, but still couldn't figure why the chief's son would be away from the main Shawnee village in the dead of winter. Suddenly, a thought that made sense crossed his mind. What if Tana-qate was trying to get home and stopped by this cave to get a break from the snow storm? If that were the case, where had he been? Why was he without any sign of a weapon?

Timar had another thought. What if Tana-qate was escaping from someone? But, who? Then, he recalled the direction from which the boy had come; he had been traveling in the same direction as he and Sequah. That meant he must have come from somewhere near Blue Lick. He decided to discuss this possibility with Sequah at daylight.

When morning light broke over the forest, it had stopped snowing. The temperature was near freezing, but the snow was already melting and falling from the tree limbs and evergreen branches as the sunrays touched them. As Timar peered from his perch at the cave entrance, the quiet, pristine vista was a wondrous sight to see. The tall graceful hemlock trees with their branches laden with new snow, rose from the banks of the stream below as if to greet the morning sun. The only sound was the trickle and gurgle of water coursing its way through the snow-covered stones in the stream bed.

Timar quietly aroused Sequah from his bed, leaving the Shawnee boy asleep. "I have been thinking," he said. "What if this one who calls himself Tana-qate, son of Black Fish, is trying to get home after being held prisoner by someone? He was not carrying any weapons, which is not how a Shawnee normally travels in the forest."

"You might be right," replied Sequah. "Maybe we should backtrack toward Blue Lick to see if we can find anything that lets us know more about this son of Black Fish."

"Good. We'll get started after we've had breakfast," said Timar. "I have a hunch we might find Tobahana and Josh somewhere back there."

Sequah found some dry wood at the rear of the cavern, and with his flint and striker, he soon had a small smokeless fire burning. Meanwhile, Timar opened his pack and took out two pewter cups, which he packed with the newly fallen snow. Soon, he had two cups of boiling water, into which he added some of Meriah's dried vegetables and chunks of dried deer meat.

When they had eaten, Timar kicked the prisoner awake and asked if he was hungry. Tana-qate grunted a refusal, saying he would not eat until he got to eat Shawnee food.

Just as they prepared to pack up and leave, a small avalanche of snow fell across the opening of the cavern. Immediately, Timar and Sequah recognized the danger and grabbed their rifles. Someone or an animal had caused the snow to turn loose. They remained quiet, ready to face whatever it was.

Suddenly, as if from out of nowhere, a tall figure appeared at the entrance. He was dressed in a long buffalo robe and carried a longrifle, from which an inverted "vee" was clearly visable on the stock.

"Josh! It's Timar and Sequah!" came the voice from the cave.

"What are you boys doing here?" was the response from the tall man.

"We came to find you and Toba. We came to help you bring the hostages home," said Timar. "Meriah is fine. We left her in good hands. Old Miskka came to the farm to see you and said he would be pleased to watch over Meriah and little Katy until we return."

"That is good news. I will be glad to see Miskka, again. But, you disappoint me Timar. I gave you specific orders to stay and take care of the farm."

"I know. I am sorry to disappoint you, but when Sequah brought the old Cherokee to see us, I saw the opportunity to come and be with you and Toba. Old Miskka said that if he were a young man, he would like to go into Kentuckee, but since he was too old to go on the trail again, he said it would be good experience for both of us. Meriah didn't want us to go at first, but after Miskka convinced her that it was time for us to become warriors, she gave us her blessing," explained Timar.

"Well, its good to see you and Sequah. I'm afraid I have some bad news concerning Tobahana. He left two nights ago to go into the Shawnee village on Wolf River. I haven't heard from him since. We were supposed to meet back here at this cave, but when he didn't return, I went back to Blue Lick to wait. That is where I lost my prisoner," said Josh.

"Then, you're the one who let Tana-qate escape," said Timar with a big smile on his face.

"How did you know about the prisoner?" asked Josh.

"We recaptured him here in this cave last night," said Timar. "He calls himself a chief's son. What do you know about him?"

"I guess he's who he claims to be. Tobahana seemed to think he was telling the truth when we first caught him. He was with a larger hunting party, but allowed us to take him without much trouble. He's been with us nearly a week, until he escaped last night."

Sequah jerked the young Shawnee to his feet and brought him from the rear of the cave. The prisoner hung his head when he faced Josh. It had been a good try, but he'd made a foolish mistake coming back to the cavern to be caught again.

"Well, I guess we'll have to make the best of this situation," said Josh. "We'll stay here for a while and see if we hear from Tobahana."

They moved the prisoner to the rear of the cave and settled down to wait. Timar and Sequah were pleased with themselves for recapturing the prisoner. Josh let them know that he was thankful and that they had possibly saved Tobahana's life.

The forest returned to its normal quietness.

Chapter Fourteen
Answers Confirmed

Tobahana couldn't believe the rough treatment they had shown to him. He was still tied to the post when the snowfall abated next morning. He was thankful that he had not frozen to death. Although they let him keep his clothing, he had to keep moving his body and stamping his feet through most of the night to keep the blood circulating. With the morning sun finally reaching him, he felt that he might survive.

They came to cut him down after the village began to stir. Two well-armed warriors slashed his bindings and pointed to one of the buildings near the main lodge. He took a few minutes to rub his arms and legs, feeling the circulation return to them. One of the guards shoved him forward, grunting an obsenity, and Tobahana complied with his command.

They pushed him into the small building and closed the doorway, leaving him alone in the empty room. Tobahana took a few minutes to survey his surroundings, finding that he was the only thing in the room. He wondered what they might have in store for him and hoped it would include some food. He hadn't eaten since the small breakfast he shared with Josh Mosby nearly two days ago.

Walking around in the small room, he soon regained enough body heat to feel warm again. After his terrible night tied to the post, Tobahana hoped he'd be able to find out about the hostages before facing the post again. He guessed that Black Fish would be coming to question him when he got around to it.

Near midday, Tobahana could hear a gathering of people outside. Through cracks in the wall of the building, he could see a number of Shawnees milling about the clearing in the center of the village. It seemed as if the entire population had congregated, including men, women and children. When he saw the two lines of warriors being formed, he knew what was about to occur. A gauntlet was about to take place and he knew what was in store for him.

The drums started up with a continual beat, as the warriors took their place in the two lines. Tobahana had never faced the gauntlet before, but he knew the seriousness of such an ordeal. Although his own people, the Senecas, never practiced this form of punishment, he had heard of it from ones who had survived the awful treatment.

As he watched the crowd grow, he knew it wouldn't be long until they came for him. He recalled one survivor who told him the only way a man could survive the gauntlet was to be brave, keep his head down, and run as swiftly as possible through the hail of clubs. Tobahana felt as strong as any man, but certainly didn't relish the thought of having to run the Shawnee gauntlet.

He saw Black Fish emerge from his quarters and walk through the parting crowd, stopping at the head of the lines. At the other end, Tobahana could see a lone figure, who he recognized as a white man with red hair and beard, dressed in a shabby buffalo robe. As he watched, two warriors brought a young naked white man through the crowd and placed him at the head of the gauntlet.

Nearby, Tobahana could see two other white men, still dressed in buckskin clothing. One was an older man, who he guessed to be John Finley. The other, taller by a head, had to be Boon. The unfortunate boy about to run the gauntlet had to be Simon Kenton.

Tobahana witnessed the whole scene while peering through a crack in the building. He was glad when the ordeal was over and he saw that the boy still lived. As the crowd dispersed, he saw Boon and Finley comforting young Kenton, who was bleeding from every part of his body. He watched as they took the white hunters back to a nearby hovel and locked them inside. The old red-haired white man was also put in the same building as the others. Now, he knew the white hunters were here and still alive.

Chapter Eleven
Simon Kenton

    After the gauntlet, the four whites were locked up again, including the old scout, Amos Boggs, who had stood at the end of the gauntlet and witnessed young Kenton's successful run. He was thankful to be in the company of other Englishmen, not having seen another white person for six months. At first, Boggs thought he had been mistakenly placed with the white hunters, and when the Shawnees didn't come back for him, he found another glimmer of hope that one day, he might be free again.

    The first priority was taking care of young Kenton's wounds. Since there was no water available to wash the blood and debris from the gaping cuts on his head and body, Boon and Finley used the only thing available. Boon removed his outer buckskin jacket and linsey-woolsy undershirt and used it to wipe the naked body of the still bleeding lad. It wasn't much comfort, but until they were given some water to cleanse the wounds, it would have to suffice.

    The boy moaned when Boon rubbed the gaping wounds. The body salt in Boon's smelly undershirt mixed with the boy's blood and stung when it touched the raw lacerations, causing him to wince at the pain. Through the whole process of cleaning up the boy, not once did he cry out. When it was done, they dressed Kenton in his own clothing and laid him in the corner of the room. Soon, the young man drifted off to sleep.

    Amos Boggs introduced himself to Boon and Finley. "Name's Boggs. Amos Boggs. I been here nigh onto six months with these savages," he said.

    When Boon and Finley looked at the skeletal frame of the old scout, they couldn't believe he was still living. There was hardly any flesh on the poor wretch, who stood there in the ragged buffalo robe. His eyes, sunken in back of blackened sockets, were rimmed with red underneath his shabby eyebrows. It was almost frightening to look him directly in the eye.

Boon was first to introduce himself to Boggs. "Name's Boon," he said, as he shook the bony hand that was extended to him. "This here is John Finley," he indicated by pointing to the man hovering over the young Kenton. "Boy's name is Simon Kenton."

"What'd ye boys do to git ketched by these heatherns?" asked Boggs.

"Well, we was hunting game 'bout twenty mile north of here when they found our camp and started shootin' at us. We fought 'em a good round or two afore we run low on shot and powder. Reckon the only thing we could do was let ourselves get captured," said Boon.

He went on to relate the entire story; how John Stewart had been killed; how three of their party made a break while he, Finley and the boy held the Shawnees off. Boon told about how they'd been taken as prisoners when their ammunition ran out.

"Don't know if the others made it or not. They lit out, heading south, hoping to find some help," continued Boon. "Guess we're lucky to still have our hair."

"Yo're right 'bout that. These Shawnee devils hate the white man worse than anythang. Don't know why they've kept me alive all these months," replied Boggs.

"Ye wouldn't have somethin' to eat, would ye?" he asked.

"Reckon not. They took our packs with what food we had. Shore am sorry," said Boon.

Boggs hung his head and looked at the dirt floor. "Jist thought I'd ask," he said. "These varmits shore are stingy with their food. I ain't 'et enough to keep a rat alive since I've been here."

Boon changed the conversation and asked Finley how the boy was doing. Young Kenton hadn't moved since he was laid in the corner of the room. Except for an occasional cough, his breathing seemed normal. Finley said it would take several days rest for the boy to recover from the ordeal.

They talked about young Kenton and how they wished

they'd never brought him on the trail. When he first joined them, he told about his family back in Prince William County and how he'd been in love with a girl named Ellen Cummins. He said another man had taken her away from him and had married her; how a year later, he caught Leachman alone in the woods and had fought and killed him. He knew he had to get away, so he headed west into the wilderness to escape from the authorities. That is where he'd met John Finley and Boon.

Well, it was too late to send the boy packing, now. He'd proven himself on the trail and had carried more than his share of the load. He had not backed down during the fight with the Shawnees, and now he had run the Shawnee gauntlet and still lived. When, and if, they got out of this mess, Boon and Finley vowed to let his family know about their brave son.

Two days they spent locked in the room without being harassed by the Indians. Young Simon was recovering as well as could be expected, without medicine or clean bandages to bind his wounds. Boon spent many hours talking to him, encouraging him to forget about the terrible beating and concentrate on getting well. It seemed to be working, as Simon gathered enough strength to spend time walking around the room and taking part in some of the conversations.

When Boggs told Simon about being from Virginia, and that he knew where Prince William County was, the boy and the old scout became friends. He told him about his being a scout for the army and that he'd been captured more than six months ago by the Shawnees. He said he'd witnessed the gauntlet before, watching while a young Englisman died trying to run the lines.

"Reckon yo're brave enough, son. T'aint many who's ever run the gauntlet and lived to tell 'bout it," he said.

The Shawnees finally brought food. It wasn't much, and not very appetizing, but they shared the corn mush and water and were thankful for it. Old Boggs said that it was more food than he'd seen in months, and ate the mush like it was a Thanksgiving feast.

"Can't say I've eaten worse," said Boon, who dished out small bowls of the gooey mixture to each man, "but it'll help keep us alive for a while longer."

The four captives could only wait to see what the Shawnees had in store for them. They were fortunate they had not been separated and moved to different locations in the village, where communication with each other would not be possible.

Finley, the oldest of the group, was nearing sixty-four years in age. He told them that all was not lost; that there was still a chance Black Fish might let them go. He tried to encourage them by saying he had been in Kentuckee a few years past and had trapped and traded with the Shawnees without any trouble. Maybe there was a chance one of the Shawnees might recognize him and speak in their behalf.

Boon was hopeful. It had been a long year for him and his family, whom he left on the Yadkin River in North Carolina. He and his family moved there from Culpeper County, Virginia in '59. He brought with him, his wife Rebecca, son, James, and a newborn daughter, Jemima, to make a new beginning in the foothills of the Great Smoky mountains.

Young Daniel was soon caught up in the exploration fever and wanted to see the Spanish territory of Florida. So, in 1765, he did just that; he lit out for the warm sunny climate, with hopes of settling there with his family. Returning home a year later, he decided Florida was not in his future plans.

When he met John Finley in the spring of '69, he couldn't resist the opportunity to see Kentuckee. He signed on with Finley and his group of hunters, expecting to make a lot of money in the trapping business. Now, it looked as if his dreams of becoming rich depended on whether the Shawnees let them live or die.

Boon admired young Kenton, who had stood the test. He liked the boy from the beginning, and hoped that someday he would be able to reward him somehow.

Chapter Fifteen
Tobahana Speaks Out

The morning following the gauntlet, Black Fish came to see Tobahana. He was in a foul mood and showed it by cursing the two guards outside the door. They were roughly pushed aside as he stomped through the doorway and into the room where Tobahana was waiting.

He came to stand in front of Tobahana, who was sitting in the center of the room meditating. Black Fish expected the Seneca to jump to his feet and acknowledge him, but Tobahana continued to sit until the Shawnee chieftain let out a guttural noise.

"You, no doubt, saw the white hunters yesterday when the young one survived the gauntlet. They are still my prisoners and will not be permitted to leave until I have taught them a lesson in Shawnee justice," said Black Fish. "Only then, will I consider releasing them if they still live."

"Surely, you don't expect to inflict more punishment on the boy?" asked Tobahana.

"At noon today, you will see more Shawnee justice. This time, you will be present," said Black Fish.

Tobahana watched as his captor turned and walked out of the room, leaving him to wonder what Black Fish had in store for him. He knew whatever it was would most likely include himself in the running of the gauntlet. He didn't relish the idea of being put through the unnessary torture and humiliation, undeserving of a Seneca warrior. Nevertheless, it looked as if there was nothing he could do to prevent the spectacle from happening.

The drumming started shortly before noon, and Tobahana could see the gathering of spectators in the clearing across the way. Hundreds of Shawnee villagers milled about, waiting for the ceremonies to begin. Two armed warriors came for him, as the lines of the gauntlet were being formed. He decided not to resist. He allowed them to take him outside, one on each side, and march him toward the center of the village.

Among the bystanders were the three white hunters and a redheaded skeleton of a man, brought forth to witness the gauntlet. They were standing at the opposite end of the two lines of club-bearing warriors and watched as Tobahana was brought forward.

Tobahana walked tall and straight between the two Shawnee guards, surveying the crowd as they neared the lines of warriors. His six-foot frame was taller than most of the other Indians gathered to see the gauntlet. Of all the people gathered, only the white hunter who stood at the end of the line was taller, whom he assumed to be Boon.

When they stopped, Black Fish appeared and the drums ceased, as he faced Tobahana. "This day, this Seneca will face the wrath of the Shawnee gauntlet because he has encroached on our hunting grounds. He says he has come to free the white hostages."

A roar of disgust rose from the bystanders. Several angry Shawnees shouted above the din, calling for the death of Tobahana. They pelted him with stones and clods of dirt as he stood unmoving at the head of the gauntlet.

Black Fish gave the order for the ceremony to begin by raising his arms high into the air. When he lowered them, two warriors stepped forward to strip Tobahana of his clothing. At this point, Tobahana reached into his shirt and produced the necklace that belonged to Tana-qate. He held it up so that everyone could get a glimpse of it. Then, he tossed the necklace to Black Fish.

The chieftain looked closely at the necklace for a brief moment and then waved off the two warriors. He walked closer to Tobahana and stood facing him, his dark piercing eyes showing a sudden hatred for this Seneca, who must know something about the disappearance of his son. He held the necklace close to Tobahana's face and shook, as if fighting back the rage to kill.

"We talk, now," was the only thing he managed to say.

Tobahana was released to follow Black Fish to his quarters. As they walked, the crowd began to disperse. He watched as the white hunters were escorted back to the building on the other side of the clearing, noticing that the young lad was recovering well.

Entering Black Fish's quarters, Tobahana was shown where to sit as two Shawnee women spread a large blanket in the center of the room. The chief pointed to the blanket and Tobahana took a seat, waiting for his host to do the same. Black Fish waved his arm and the two women departed, leaving only him and the Seneca to face each other. He removed his buffalo robe and took a seat directly facing Tobahana. After studying his guest for several minutes, he dangled the necklace in Tobahana's face and spoke.

"You will tell me about this necklace," said Black Fish, and crossed his arms to wait for an answer.

Tobahana was slow to respond, allowing Black Fish a few minutes to anticipate the news of his son, Tana-qate. The necklace was the key to the release of the prisoners, and he wanted to be very careful about how to best use the key. He stared directly into the black eyes of his captor, and when he figured he had waited long enough, he responded.

"I am called Tobahana of the Seneca."

Before he could continue, Black Fish retorted, "I know who you are, Seneca. You're the one who killed the great Scarface. Your fame is known in all Shawnee villages as the one who ended the life of one of out greatest warriors."

"It is true that I tried to kill Scarface. We fought many times during his time, but I am not the one who sent him to the spirit world," replied Tobahana.

Black Fish had been one of the lesser chiefs in the battle near Painted Mountain when the Shawnees were defeated. He had barely escaped with a few of his own warriors to spread the story of how Scarface had been killed. When he returned to Wolf River, he told of the battle and how they had been defeated by a smaller Cherokee force, led by a Seneca and white man. It was generally believed that Scarface had been killed by the Seneca, who was his long-time enemy.

Tobahana continued to explain, "The white man who killed Scarface is the one who has your son, Tana-qate. I am here to offer exchange of your son for the three white hunters who were taken at their camp, near the salt lick."

Black Fish tried to suppress the anger welling up inside. His face suddenly became contorted with bulging blood vessels and eyes so full of hatred, even Tobahana was concerned. His mouth twisted into a grimacing snarl as he tried to speak, but couldn't spit the words out. He glared directly at the tall warrior who sat watching him. Finally, when he regained his composure, he spoke to Tobahana.

"You do not know how close you are to dying," he managed to sputter. "If you have harmed my son, I will personally skin you alive."

Tobahana knew he meant it. He did not speak for several minutes, letting Black Fish steep in his thoughts, watching the expression on his face change from bitter hatred to an imploring worry.

"If Black Fish wants to see Tana-qate again, he will not harm me or the white hunters. The one who has your son will not hesitate to end his life if I do not return with your prisoners. He will wait for only one more day," said Tobahana.

Black Fish rose from his seat and began pacing around the room, many thoughts running through his mind. He was not ready to release the white men until they had been punished, yet, if he kept them more than another day, he knew he would never see Tana-qate again. This Seneca, who now held the upper hand, would surely allow the one who had him to take his life.

Many questions crossed his mind. What if he released the prisoners, only to find his son already dead? What would the council say when he took it upon himself to release the white men? Would they overrule him and retain the prisoners, causing Tana-qate's death? He was suddenly in a quandary as to what course he should take.

When he stopped pacing and took a seat again, he asked Tobahana one last question. "Does my son still live?" he asked with head bowed.

"Tana-qate was still living two days ago. I feel sure that he is still a prisoner of the white man who is my brother-in-law. If he does not hear from me, he will assume that I have been killed and will take the next step, which is to take the life of Tana-qate. That is why you must release me. I will return to where I left your son in his care, and make plans for the exchange," said Tobahana, hoping that Black Fish would agree to release him.

Black Fish rose from his seat and put on his long buffalo robe. As he turned to leave, he spoke one more time to Tobahana.

"You will stay here until I have talked with the council of leaders. One thing more," he said, "Do not try to escape."

Tobahana was relieved that things were going as well as they were. He hoped to have the prisoners freed and on their way home soon. His only worry at the moment was that Josh still had Tana-qate in his care, and was still waiting for him back at the hunter's old camp. If Black Fish could convince the tribal council that freeing the prisoners would bring his son back, then he could be on his way in the next few hours.

He knew they would try to follow him by sending scouts out ahead of his release. No doubt, they would lie in wait until he passed and follow him. It presented a real problem, but with a little ingenuity and luck, he figured he could outwit his pursuers and make his way back to Josh and Tana-qate.

An hour later, Black Fish reentered his quarters where he found Tobahana just as he'd left him. "You will go now. But, if you do not return in one day's time with my son, I will make the white prisoners beg for death."

"I will leave with my possessions," said Tobahana. "Black Fish has made a wise decision. I will be back with Tana-qate before the sun sets tomorrow. Do not send your warriors to follow me, or I will have to kill them."

Black Fish called two of his braves to fetch Tobahana's

rifle and possibles pouch. When they returned, he walked with the Seneca to the edge of the village.

"If you do not return by sundown tomorrow, you will not be allowed to enter my village. The lives of the white hunters are now in your hands. If you do not bring my son back, they will pay the price for his life," said Black Fish, making sure that Tobahana understood the seriousness of the matter.

Tobahana did not acknowledge what Black Fish said. He merely kept on walking, leaving the Shawnee chief standing alone at the edge of the village. Moving away from the settlement and into the snow covered forest, he soon disappeared from sight.

Because of the circumstances, Tobahana left the Shawnee village without having contact with any of the hostages. He had hoped to meet with them to check on their condition, especially that of the young lad who had run the gauntlet, but time would not permit him to waste precious hours.

Up ahead, he knew the Shawnee scouts would be waiting to track him. Black Fish would not have passed up the opportunity to try to free Tana-quate and retain possession of the hostages. With that in mind, Tobahana decided not to go directly back to the meeting place. His first objective would be losing the scouts.

Chapter Sixteen
A Plan to Escape

"What do you think is going on?" Boon asked when they were put back in their holding room.

"Looks like that Indian did something to get out of running the gauntlet. I think we were supposed to witness his beating in the gauntlet; otherwise, why would Black Fish show his hostages to a stranger?" Finley responded.

"At least someone besides a Shawnee knows we're here," said Boon.

"Aye," said the old scout, "If I recollect correctly, that Injun wore the markin's of a Seneca. The Shawnee and Seneca are long-time enemies. Reckon that one's carryin' his lucky rabbit's foot."

"It must have been that necklace he tossed to Black Fish. Did you notice how quickly he changed his mind about the gauntlet?" asked Boon.

"There is a chance he is talking to Black Fish about our release," said Finley. "Maybe the others did get back and tell what happened here."

"We'll just have to wait and see," replied Boon.

The four of them decided that if they were to get out of their situation, they needed a plan. Now that the old scout was with them, he could give them valuable information that might help in the formulation of an escape. Young Simon would not be much help, since he was still hurting from the beating he received. It looked like it was left to Finley and Boon to come up with a plan.

Between the three of them, they decided to share some of their clothing with Boggs, who had nothing but the tattered buffalo robe to keep him warm. Boon was the first to remove his outer garment and take off his linen shirt, which he gave to the old man. Finley removed his buckskin pants, shed his linsey-woolsey underwear, and offered them to Boggs. They were unable to share their boots, but Boon removed his long stockings. They were too large, but the old scout accepted them and quickly put them on. Young Kenton wanted to contribute, but they told him he would need his clothing in case he got feverish.

Old Boggs was most appreciative of the gifts and wasted no time putting on the underwear and linen shirt. He looked lost in the loose garments, which draped over his skeleton-like figure. Tearing a strip of cloth from the bottom of the long shirt, he fashioned a belt and tied it tightly around his waist. He stood there barefoot and proud of his new clothing.

That afternoon, they sat closely in one corner of the room and discussed a plan for their escape.

"We need to do it during the night when we're less likely to be seen," said Finley. "If we wait until Black Fish decides to hold another gauntlet, or maybe something worse, we may never have the opportunity to escape."

"We must wait a while longer for young Kenton to regain his strength," interjected Boon. "I doubt if he could get very far in his condition."

Amos Boggs spoke, "Aye. We must all go together. If one of us remains, he will be tortured to death."

"Then, whatever we decide must include all of us," said Boon. "I'm all for waiting a few days 'til Simon is able to travel."

Finley, who had been in charge of the hunting expedition, agreed. He was not one who would abandon a friend.

"We will wait. While we're waiting, we will work on the plan," he said.

Chapter Seventeen
Tobahana's Trail

After leaving the Shawnees, Tobahana disappeared into the forest. He could see the village from a distance, and waited for them to send a scouting party to follow him. An hour passed as he watched without anyone leaving the village. He was beginning to think Black Fish might have no intention of following him, when he saw the first of three scouts pick up his trail at the edge of the forest.

He watched as the first brave easily found his tracks in the snow. The trail he was leaving was not hard to find and the tracker came toward the forest, soon to be joined by two others. They were not interested in catching up to Tobahana, figuring he would lead them straight to the chief's son, so they lingered around the fresh tracks in the snow.

Tobahana knew he could not take a direct route to the meeting place, and so he decided to mislead the scouting party. It would not be an easy task, since Black Fish had no doubt hand-picked the members of the party. They were probably the best trackers in the village and he would have a hard time losing them in the snow-covered forest.

He moved away from the Shawnee town and headed south. As he reached the top of a high ridge, he stopped to see if they were on his trail. Far in the distant valley he could make out three small figures steadily coming onward. Tobahana knew they would not overtake him until he reached the place where Tana-qate was being held. He took time to set his plan in motion to elude them.

Along the peak of the south ridge, he found what he was looking for. A long stretch of stone outcroppings, wind-blown and free of snow, lined the southern slope, and ran along the full length of the ridge. He climbed the first outcropping, leaving his tracks of snow residue on the stones. As he advanced farther along the ridge, jumping from stone to stone, his tracks gradually became undetectable. When he thought he'd gone far enough to cause his trackers some concern, he doubled back to where he began on the outcroppings.

He sat on a stone and removed his boots. Barefoot and carrying his boots, he jumped to another stone and started off in the opposite direction, making sure that he didn't touch any snow along the outcroppings. When he had gone nearly a mile along the ridge, he stopped and put on his boots. He lowered himself over the edge of the rocky ledge. Finding a small cavern underneath it, he decided to stop and wait to see if the scouts were able to pick up his trail.

As he explored the small cavern, he noticed an opening at the rear, barely large enough to allow a man to crawl through it. The opening was formed when the cavern walls had collapsed long ago. He could not see beyond the first few feet, so he decided to explore it later.

Tobahana knew time was quickly slipping away and wished his persuers would soon get over their little game of hide and seek. He doubted if they knew he was aware of them in the beginning, but when they found that his tracks had disappeared, they would surely know that he was eluding them. Much time would be lost because of their efforts to solve the tracking dilemma.

While he waited on the trackers, he considered how far he was away from Josh and his prisoner. Blue Lick was at least twenty miles from the Shawnee village, and he was now about five miles south of it, in the opposite direction. That meant he had at least fifty miles to travel to get back to Black Fish before the following sundown. He was not worried that he could travel that far in one day; only that if he kept being dogged by the Shawnee scouts, it would cost him valuable time.

Above the cavern overhang, he could hear the three scouts as they talked. From their conversation, he understood that they had lost his trail. One of them said the trail disappeared as if the Seneca had turned into a spirit, leaving no tracks at all. Another said it was impossible to disappear without leaving a trace. After much discussion, they decided to retrace the ridge top to check the trail again.

When he was sure they were gone, Tobahana decided to explore the opening in the rear of the cavern. Squeezing through the small crack in the wall, he was surprised to see that it opened up on the other side. He could barely see in the darkness, the only light coming from the crack through which he had just emerged.

After his eyes became more adjusted to the darkness, he could see that he was in a large room. Stepping cautiously away from the opening, he moved toward the interior of the cavern, discovering that the floor sloped downward, toward the other side of the room. Without a light, he dared not venture further and returned to opening, where he crawled out to the overhanging cliff.

He could not hear anything except the quietness of the snow-covered forest, as he listened for sounds of the scouting party. It seemed as if they had given up the hunt for his trail. He waited beneath the overhang for the better part of an hour, deciding they had most likely returned to the Shawnee village.

Tobahana knew he was still in a predicament. Retracing his own trail would only take him back to the place where he first climbed onto the stony outcroppings. He couldn't leave his hiding place without leaving tracks that could easily be found in the snow.

There was no use to leave his hiding place until after darkness fell upon the mountains, so with a few hours to wait, he thought of the cavern and decided to explore further into its depths. This time, he fabricated a torchlight to assist his journey into the darkness.

Taking a stick of dry wood from underneath the overhang, he applied some bear grease from the tin in his possibles pouch. When the end of the wood was thoroughly saturated, he tied several strands of buckskin, torn from the inside of his buffalo overcoat and applied more bear grease. Then, he used his flint and punk from his pack to start a small fire which he used to light the torch. In a few minutes, he had a small torchlight that would serve him in the darkness of the cavern.

He knew the torch wouldn't last long, so he began to immediately explore the other side of the crack in the wall. As he entered the large room, he noticed that the limestone walls were high enough to walk upright. Cautiously, Tobahana made his way to the rear of the cavern. What he saw made him stop and inspect the area more closely.

On the rear wall, he noticed several strange markings. They looked as if they represented animals which he had never seen. One of them was larger than the others, and looked like a weird, fat buffalo with two long, upturned horns on either side of a long, downward curving snout. Another cat-like figure showed two long teeth projecting from its open mouth. Several bison, which Tobahana recognized, were also drawn along with the other paintings.

He knew that these animal paintings were very old, and were probably put there by the ancient ones many centuries ago. As he surveyed the work of his ancient predecessors there on the limestone wall in front of him, he was awestruck at the details of the animal representations. This was surely a sacred cavern, he thought to himself, wondering if he were the only person to view them in hundreds of years. He wished Josh Mosby was here with him to see the beautiful artwork.

Tobahana suddenly remembered his original objective and resumed his search of the cavern. At the end of the large room, another small passage was visible and he decided to explore further. Leaving the larger room, he journeyed down the smaller passage as it wound along steadily downward through the bowels of the mountain ridge. Somewhere up ahead, he could hear the trickle of water.

As he approached the end of the passageway, he entered another small room, where a freshwater stream spilled from a crack in the limestone. After tasting the water and finding it very palatable, he cupped his hands and drank from the spring. He followed the flow of the spring as it spewed over the precipices within the cavern, on its downward journey to the outside world.

Tobahana's torch was beginning to burn out when he saw a small ray of light up ahead. He hurried onward, still able to walk along the stream, which was now starting to level out before it reached the opening in the mountain. He was glad that he wouldn't have to retrace his steps through the cavern, considering it would have left him stranded on top of the ridge.

At the end of the trip through the cavernous descent from the ridge, Tobahana found no visible evidence of the trackers as he looked over the snow-covered area near the exiting stream. He made no effort to venture from the concealment of the cavern, waiting until darkness came before resuming his trip back to Blue Lick.

The stream provided the way for him to conceal his sign as he ventured out of his hiding place. In the shallow stream bed, Tobahana waded the water, careful not to step out of the water. He made slow progress, stepping carefully along. He could not allow the slightest sign of his passing.

Sometime near midnight, he guessed that he had traveled nearly five miles downstream from the cavern. His feet were terribly cold, although his waterproof boots worked very well to keep his feet dry. He decided it was worth the risk to leave the stream and make his way northward again.

The snow made traveling slow work, as Tobahana traversed ridge after ridge through the night. Although there was no visible moon, the snow provided enough light for him to see his way. It was nearing daylight when he found the old camp at Blue Lick.

He found no sign of Josh Mosby near the camp ruins, leaving him puzzled that his brother-in-law was not there at their agreed-upon meeting place. With no way to know for sure that Josh had been there, he decided to look outside of the perimeter of the camp for some clue that would lead him to his partner.

As he scouted in wider circles around the camp, he came across several fresh tracks in the snow. It seemed as if the

Shawnees had returned to the camp and was probably the reason he could not find Josh and Tana-qate. He continued to look around for some positive sign that Josh had returned with his prisoner to the old camp.

Underneath the grove of hemlocks on the ridge north of the salt lick, Tobahana found tracks in the snow. There were two sets of footprints, one set almost snowed over, representing an early departure from the hemlock grove. The other set was made from a much larger boot, and he immediately took it to be Josh's prints. If he was right, it looked as if Tana-qate had escaped.

Tobahana wasted no time in following the trail. He knew the tracks would eventually lead him to Josh, but what worried him was the fact that Josh, himself, was tracking the escaped prisoner, Tana-qate. If the young Shawnee was able to get back to the main village, the lives of the hostages would not be worth anything. When he reached the ridge where the blazed tree with the arrow stood, he saw that two sets of tracks had discovered the marking. If these tracks were made by the Shawnee scouts, he knew Josh was in trouble.

It looked as if all of the tracks were headed in the direction of the Shawnee village. Following the tracks was easier than he expected. That is, until they became wind-blown, and soon disappeared as he reached the higher mountain range. When he had no trail to follow, his only option was to go back to the village. There, he fully expected to find Josh a prisoner of the Shawnees.

Halfway there, he decided to stop again at the small cavern where he and Josh had camped several days ago. As he approached, he noticed that the tracks had reappeared and were converged at the entrance. He studied the tracks for several minutes, noting that they all headed into the cave. He saw none leading away from it.

He didn't know what he'd find in the small cave, so he made his way very carefully to the entrance. When he peered into the opening, what he saw brought a big smile to his face. There in the rear of the cavern were Josh, Timar and two others whom he recognized immediately. He let them know is identity by calling out.

"Timar! What are you and Sequah doing here?" he asked loud and very seriously.

Overjoyed, Timar was on his feet and rushed forward to grab his brother. Tobahana quickly sidestepped and Timar went sprawling headlong through the cave entrance. Josh and Sequah joined Tobahana and watched as Timar slid down the slope, ending up on his backside in the middle of the stream. Everyone laughed as Timar slowly recovered from his embarrassment and climbed back up the snow-covered slope to the cave.

Water still dripping from his clothes, he grasped Tobahana's arm and said, "Sequah and I followed you and Josh to help you bring the hostages back. It is a good thing we did. We recaptured the chief's son in this cave last evening."

"Good. Time is quickly slipping away. We have to get the boy to Black Fish before sundown. But first, we must have a plan so we won't get ourselves captured," said Tobahana.

Without wasting time on greetings, the four of them gathered at the rear of the cave to discuss the plan to deliver Tanaqate.

Chapter Eighteen
Trading Prisoners

Now that Timar and Sequah were part of the group, Tobahana and Josh filled them in on what had taken place in the last few days. Tobahana told them of his meeting with Black Fish and that he had seen the prisoners, but was unable to talk with them. He told them of witnessing the gauntlet, and how the young prisoner had survived the ordeal.

Josh related how he let Tana-qate slip away from him back at Blue Lick, and almost spoiled the only chance to free the prisoners. He felt bad about his mistake, but forgave himself when he found Tana-qate in the hands of Timar and Sequah.

The problem facing them now, was how to exchange prisoners with the Shawnees without getting themselves captured. Black Fish was a shrewd chief. He would not stand for any trickery or let the hostages go without first dictating the particulars of the exchange. They needed to control the situation instead of letting Black Fish hold the upper hand.

After much discussion, Tobahana suggested that he and Timar return to the Shawnees without the prisoner. They still had a few hours before sundown. If they hurried, they might get Black Fish to make the exchange somewhere outside the village where they would stand a better chance of not being taken themselves. If things worked out, they might get out of the situation without incident.

Josh and Sequah agreed to go with them as far as the edge of the forest near the village to lend support, in case it was needed. They would keep the young Tana-qate in their care while Tobahana talked to Black Fish. As long as they had the young Shawnee in their possession, Josh felt that they might be able to convince the chief to comply with Tobahana's plan.

They parted before getting to the village. Tobahana and Timar, went on ahead to see Black Fish. Josh and Sequah, along with their prisoner, found a secure hiding place in the forest and waited on the result of Tobahana's encounter with the chief of the Shawnees. They kept Tana-qate gagged, but as comfortable as possible, considering he was also bound hand and foot.

While they waited, Josh suggested that some kind of fortification would be useful if Tobahana had to leave the village with the Shawnees after him. At least they could give him some cover fire from behind a make-shift barricade. Maybe he would be coming with Black Fish and the prisoners. If that were the case, they still might need the fortification for protection in case things didn't go well.

At once, he and Sequah began to gather brush and dead logs from the surrounding area. They hastily constructed a defensive structure that would serve them as protection if it came to a fight. The snow made their work more difficult, as they raked the area with their feet to locate logs and fallen timber. They carried the timbers to one location and piled them up to form a protective barrier. This would also give them a place to shoot from if necessary. When it was finished, they sat with Tana-qate and waited on Tobahana.

Tobahana and Timar walked directly into the village, where they were met by several of Black Fish's personal warriors. They made no attempt to disarm them. For reasons unknown to them, they were led to the building which housed the four prisoners, instead of being taken to Black Fish. They were going to meet the prisoners, at last.

Tobahana was quite surprised when they entered the room. There with the hostages, was Black Fish himself, talking to Boon and Finley. He was quick to recognize the Seneca and motioned for him to be seated with the others.

Boon and Finley didn't understand the meaning of Tobahana's presence, and asked Black Fish who he was.

"This Seneca has come to take you away from Wolf River if he has kept his part of the agreement. He told me he will trade my son for your worthless hides," scoffed Black Fish.

Tobahana refused to take a seat and stood with his rifle cradled in his arms. He waited for Black Fish to finish his conversation with the hostages, who seemed to be unaware of the agreement between him and the chief. They listened as Black Fish continued.

"If the Seneca has done his part, you will be set free before sundown this day. I will give you one last warning," he said with a stern voice. "Do not enter Shawnee land in Kentuckee again. The next time will be your last time. My warriors will have no mercy. Your scalps will hang from their lodges."

After he finished speaking to the hostages, Black Fish turned his attention to Tobahana. "What does this Seneca have to say?" he asked, as his eyes noticed Tobahana's young brother. "Who is this with you?"

Tobahana tried to be as calm as possible and spoke with a soft voice to the brash Shawnee chief. "Your son will be here before the sun leaves the sky. I have made arrangements."

Tobahana answered his last question, "This Timar, brother of Tobahana of the Senecas. He has come with me to help in the exchange of your prisoners."

Timar stood tall and proudly, as if he were one of the important members of the rescue party. He was letting the chief know that he was a Seneca warrior, although he looked more like an Englishman, with his short haircut and racoon skin hat.

"So, you have brought your little brother," quipped Black Fish. "Does the great Seneca warrior need help?"

"Timar is part of the plan to rescue the hostages and return your son," replied Tobahana. "Without him, it would be impossible for me to return Tana-qate."

He did not want to eleborate further by telling him that Timar had recaptured Tana-qate, nor did he want to reveal his exchange plan until the time was right for it. He and Timar had worked out a feasible plan with Josh before coming to the Shawnee village, and the timing of the exchange would be critical. It had to take place just before sundown.

Tobahana wanted a chance to talk to the men he had come

to rescue, but it didn't look like he was going to get the opportunity. Instead, Black Fish asked him to come to his lodge for more talk. Perhaps this would give him the opportunity to tell Black Fish how the exchange of prisoners was going to happen. He followed the chief out of the prisoners' room and walked with him to his quarters.

Timar stayed with the prisoners, who were anxious to hear of the exchange, and gathered around him to ask questions. He was reluctant at first to give away the particulars of the trade, but told them that he was only here to assist his brother in making sure that nothing went wrong. Boon and Finley were pleased when he told them about the three hunters who escaped and found their home back in Virginia. They were saddened to hear of the death of William Cool, who had died as the result of an arrow wound.

"Who is this Seneca that has come to rescue us?" Boon asked. "It is rare that an Indian would risk his life to save white men."

"Tobahana is not alone. There is also a white man, who is one of the greatest longknives on the frontier. He is also my brother-in-law. His name is Josh Mosby and he is holding the chief's son to trade for your lives," said Timar boastfully. "Josh Mosby is the man who killed the evil Shawnee, Scarface, several years ago."

"We have heard of this Scarface. He is the one who caused a lot of deaths along the frontier about ten years ago," said Finley.

"Yes, he is the one. It took Josh and Tobahana nearly a year to track him down and put an end to the Shawnee raids," replied Timar. "I was only a boy then, but I was with them when Scarface was sent to the spirit world of the damned."

"What does this brother of yours have in mind?" asked Boon.

"That will depend on Black Fish and whether he wants his son back," said Timar. "Tobahana and I think his plan is sound. It will happen before sundown is all that I can tell you."

They noticed that Timar still retained his arms, which included his longrifle, stag-handled knife and tomahawk. The Shawnees were not worried that he would try anything, since they were on guard outside the building. He and Tobahana were similarly armed and allowed to keep their weapons.

He noticed the fourth prisoner and turned his attention to ragged redhead. At first, Amos Boggs was afraid to talk to Timar, since he was an Indian, but when he heard the conversation between Timar and the others, he became more friendly.

Boggs related how long he'd been a prisoner of the Shawnees. "Reckon I been here nigh on to seven or eight months," he said. "Them varmits nearly kilt me several times. They even had me burnt at the stake onc't."

He continued to reflect on his imprisonment, "I ain't had a good meal to eat since I been here. They don't share good food with prisoners. All I been able to git is scraps and a gourd of water now and then."

Timar felt sorry for the old scout and wondered why he had been so mistreated. "I guess you're the worst case of mistreatment I've ever seen," he said, looking over the bony body of Boggs, beginning with his bare, blackened feet.

"I'm sure that Tobahana is working out a deal with Black Fish to get you released, also. We did not know that another white man was being held here," he said with pity.

When he turned his attention to the young boy lying in the corner of the room, Timar asked them what had happened to him.

"This boy is Simon Kenton. Black Fish made him run the gauntlet and he's recovering from the whipping he received at the hands of those savages," said Finley. "Never thought a youngster could live after such a beating. It looks like he's going to make it, though."

"He'll have to muster some energy to leave with us," said Timar. "When we leave and Black Fish gets his son back, he will send a war party after us. We will have to travel fast and stay ahead of them."

After hearing this, Simon Kenton said, "I will be ready. Just tell me what to do."

During the afternoon, Boon and Finley questioned Timar about how they had managed to capture the chief's son. When he told them of Tana-qate's escape and recapture, they said that was a good sign they would be freed. It was doubtful that Black Fish would let anyone loose if he was not getting his son back.

Meanwhile, Tobahana and Black Fish sat in his lodge and talked. Their tribes had been natural enemies for many years- since the Shawnees were kicked out of the Iroquois League of Nations for their belligerence to the other members of the league. Their war-like attitude to both Indian and whites had remained constant during the years after they migrated westward into the Ohios. Now they had a new enemy: the white settlers who were leaving the east to find new homes and farms west of the Blue Mountains.

As the year of seventeen sixty-nine drew to a close, many of the Indian tribes had made peace with the white settlers, allowing them to establish farms and villages in the north, and in the western part of Virginia. The Shawnees were the only tribe which did not recognize any of the peace treaties, and remained a constant threat to the new immigrants. The British Army was constantly putting down uprisings and supressing the renegade Shawnees whenever they could catch them, but the vast frontier made it impossible to retain the peace.

Now that war with the British was looming on the horizon, the Shawnees and other tribes to the north had made talks with them, and would most likely fight on the side of the British. This left men like Tobahana and his brother, who had allied themselves with the British, having to make a choice.

When the war came, and it looked as if it was imminent, Tobahana would have to declare his loyalty. In times past, he had worked for the British on the frontier, and had even grown fond of some of their fort commanders. At the present time, he was still in their employment.

Black Fish would have no problem making his decision.

He hated the white settlers, and if he had his way, he would kill every one of them. He knew the British would welcome him as an ally.

Tobahana was the first to speak. "Black Fish has been gracious to allow us to take the white hostages back. I will see that Tana-qate is returned unharmed as we agreed."

"It must be so, or you and the whites will die," said Black Fish. "There will be no change in my demands. You will bring my son back to me by sundown."

"I will tell you my plan for the exchange. There will be no change in my demands, also," said Tobahana, looking the chief directly in the eye.

"What is the Seneca's plan?" asked Black Fish.

Tobahana did not trust Black Fish for one second. He knew that if he got a chance, he would have the hostages killed before the exchange could be completed. So, he decided to lay out his demands and see if Black Fish responded favorably.

"First, the white hunters will be given back their weapons and equipment. They will need protection while they return to their homes. Next, I want the old one with the red hair freed with them. He is of no use to you." spoke a stern-faced Tobahana. "I will lead the prisoners out of here myself, and expect you to honor your agreement. Then, I do not want you to send your warriors after us. If they try to recapture the white hunters, many Shawnee will die for nothing."

"This Seneca makes brave talk. I, Black Fish, chief of the Wolf River Shawnees, will let the prisoners go at my discretion. However, I have given you my word that if you return Tana-qate unharmed, I will let you take them," said the chief.

"What is the rest of your plan?" he asked.

"The exchange will take place at sundown. When the sun touches the mountain top west of your village, we will trade prisoners," said Tobahana.

"Then it is settled. I will wait until sundown," replied Black Fish.

Tobahana was granted permission to join Timar and the others and he bade Black Fish farewell. When he entered the room of hostages, he saw that they looked at him with a different attitude. He was greeted by Boon and Finley with respect. They now had hope.

During the next two hours before sundown, Tobahana told them how the exchange would take place. He emphasized that they give no cause for the Shawnees to renege on their agreement. He told them that he'd asked for their weapons to be returned, but hadn't gotten a response from Black Fish. Maybe he would allow it before they left.

Within the hour, two Shawnee braves entered with arms loaded with rifles and equipment. The hunters immediately looked through the pile, separating it to find their own belongings. Happy to have their equipment back, they thanked Tobahana for his part in convincing Black Fish.

The next hour was spent checking and cleaning their longrifles, loading them for later use, if necessary. Everyone except Boggs got their belongings back. With some apprehension, he was given young Kenton's rifle until Kenton was well enough to use it. Boggs acted as if he wanted to rush out and take the whole Shawnee village on, but soon settled down and sat with young Kenton in the corner.

Tobahana noted his conduct and feared that he might regret the dicision to let him have the rifle. He also asked the group to go through their things and find some clothing for Boggs. Now that they had their belongings back, each of them had an extra change of clothing in their packs. Boon's clothes were too big. Young Kenton's were too small, so Finley shared his extra set of buckskins with the old scout, who was elated to get the clothes. Finley also provided an extra set of moccasins, which Boggs was able to wear.

As time for the exchange drew closer, Tobahana went over last minute instructions. "When you start walking away from the village, don't look back. Keep walking forward. I will be with you until we are into the forest. Timar will stay here with the chief until we are out of sight. At that point, Josh Mosby will send the chief's son across the opening. Timar will leave from here at the same time. They should pass each other when they reach the center of the clearing."

Tobahana continued, "If everything goes well with the exchange, we should put some distance between us and the Shawnees as fast as possible. Black Fish will try to recapture you if he can, by sending out a war party. We must be ready to protect ourselves."

Boon and Finley were glad that this Seneca had taken the initiative to rescue them. They liked his plan and told him they thought it would work.

"If anyone lags behind, they will be caught," said Tobahana. "I have scouted area and know which way we will travel. It will be rough on young lad and Boggs. Our lives will depend on how well they keep up."

"Ye don't have to worry 'bout me," interjected Boggs. "When I git outta this hell-hole, I ain't gonna give them varmits 'nother chance to torture me no more."

Tobahana was still worried about the two keeping up, but he didn't want to let it show. If they were willing, somehow he would help them make it.

The Shawnees came for them just before sundown. Followed by a large contingent of warriors, they were marched to the edge of the village facing the clearing. Black Fish was already there, waiting for them. Tobahana stopped to converse one last time with him.

"When we reach forest, my friends will release Tana-qate. To show that we are trusting Black Fish, my own brother will stay with you until your son is released. Both will start across the opening at the same time. Timar and Tana-qate will pass in the center of the clearing. I will have your son in my sights until my brother safely reaches other side. Is that agreeable to you?"

"You seem to have it worked out," replied Black Fish. "I will agree, but if you make the mistake of double-crossing me, I will not hesitate to send my warriors after you."

"We will leave now," spoke Tobahana as he motioned to the others.

Black Fish stood boldly, wrapped in his long buffalo robe, and watched the group of hunters walk by him. He couldn't resist saying one last thing. "You are fortunate, Red Hair. I would have fed your carcass to the wolves."

Boggs grinned at him as he passed. He wished for the opportunity to face Black Fish again, when he had his strength back. He hated the Shawnee chief more than anyone he had ever known.

The group of hunters started across the clearing, leaving Timar behind with the Shawnees. He watched them make their way across the clearing and hoped they would reach the other side without trouble. He also felt insecure in the presence of the large group of warriors who had gathered near him. Tobahana had asked to be the one to stay, but Timar insisted, saying it was a way to prove himself as a warrior. Tobahana finally relented and let him be the one to remain.

As Tobahana and the hunters reached the forest, Josh appeared from his concealment and greeted them. "I see you have done it. We were beginning to worry."

"Is Tana-qate ready? asked Tobahana.

"He's ready. We had to keep him restrained. He knows we're close to his home and his father," said Josh. "How did Timar like the idea of staying back?"

"He knows the danger. Timar will do what we asked of him," replied Tobahana.

After the group of hunters were safely in the forest, Tobahana untied Tana-qate and told him how the rest of the trade was to take place.

"You will start walking toward your village. Do not run or I will put a rifle ball in your back," he said, trying to instill some fear in the young Shawnee. "My brother will start at same time. You should pass each other in center of field. Just remember, I will have you in my sights until you reach other side."

When he had loosed Tana-qate's bindings, he motioned for him to start. He hoped the boy understood the importance of doing just as he had instructed. Tana-qate walked away from his captors, not bothering to look back to see if Tobahana had his rifle aimed at him.

Josh, in the meantime, charged the hunters to follow him as fast as they could travel. He led them away from the Shawnee village, heading directly south, toward the rendevous site he and Tobahana had discussed earlier. Only the old scout, Boggs, had a hard time keeping up.

Tobahana watched as Tana-qate neared the center of the opening. He could see Timar coming forward alone to meet the young Shawnee. Everything seemed to be working out the way he intended.

As the two young braves met in the middle of the opening, they stopped and faced each other. Tobahana couldn't hear what was being said, but he guessed they were exchanging their farewells. As Timar started onward, the unexpected happened.

Tana-qate suddenly turned and threw himself into the back of Timar with such force that both went down. Timar tried to free himself from the attacking youngster, but was unable to regain his feet. Both rolled over and over, trying to gain an advantage. Tobahana watched from the other side of the field and could do nothing to help his little brother.

Suddenly, from the other side, a wall of angry, shouting Shawnee warriors rushed toward the two struggling youngsters. Tobahana watched in disbelief as they reached the center of the field and surrounded Timar and Tana-qate. A loud roar from the melee of warriors told Tobahana that his brother was now the prisoner of the Shawnees.

There was nothing he could do to rescue Timar. There were too many Shawnees to even attempt it. He could only stand there and watch, as they gloried in their victory.

Knowing that he couldn't do anything to save Timar at the time, Tobahana turned his attention to the rescued hunters.

His first priority was to help Josh get them back to civilization. He would have to deal with Black Fish later.

He caught up with Josh and Sequah at the rendevous point and told them of the disaster that had taken place after they departed. Josh and Sequah could not believe what he was telling them.

"Poor Timar. I hope he can last until we can find a way to rescue him," said Sequah. "He was my best friend."

"We'll get him back," said Josh. "We can't do anything at the moment, but we'll be back to rescue him. I only hope the Shawnees will let him live until then."

Tobahana could see the concern of Josh and Sequah. He wanted nothing more than to go back and fight Black Fish's warriors, but knew it would be futile. Instead, he turned his attention to the group of hunters.

"First, we have to get these men to safety. Black Fish will be on our trail at sunrise. We must put some miles between us before we are safe," he said.

Chapter Nineteen
The Flight

The flight from the Shawnees was an event the hostages would never forget. Traveling through the rough terrain was a task that only the experienced hunter could manage during daylight hours. It was completely dark now and they were trying to put as much distance as possible between themselves and the Shawnees, who were sure to be on their trail come sunup.

Tobahana produced a rawhide rope and told each one to tie it around his waist. That way, it would keep them together and no one would get lost or be left behind. He led the way as they crossed the first of several ridges, leading them south toward home and freedom from the savages.

He had a plan, but hadn't told anyone about it, yet. If he could get the hunters back to the cavern with the animal paintings without being caught, they might be able to hide and wait until the war party gave up. It was a long shot, considering the tracks they were making in the snow. He knew the Shawnees would easily discover the tracks and have no trouble tracking them. If they could reach the stream leading to the ridge with the cavern, there might be a chance to evade the pursuers. When they stopped for a breather, Tobahana called Josh for a conference to explain his plan.

"When we get to a stream somewhere up ahead, I want you to take charge of hunters and lead them to cave I found yesterday. It is well concealed. Large enough for all of you to hide for as long as it takes to get Shawnee war party discouraged," said Tobahana.

"What are you going to do?" asked Josh.

"I will try to get war party off your trail. Then, I will come to cave if I do not get caught," said Tobahana. "If you do not hear from me in two days, you must leave cave and get the hunters to safety. You have enough food in your packs to survive for at least two more days."

Tobahana continued, "When we get to stream, we will go separate ways. You take hunters upstream. I will make much sign and lead Shawnees downstream. Since there is still much snow on ground, you must wade stream. Make sure that hunters do not leave tracks. You will find entrance to cave where stream comes from mountain. It is small opening and hard to get inside. You will follow stream inside mountain. It will take you to large room in cave."

Josh wanted to go with Tobahana, but knew he had to get the hunters to safety. "I will do as you say. I hope the others will understand how much danger we're still in."

"If they do not, they will lose their hair," emphasized Tobahana.

"I think Boon will be the one to lead them up the stream. I will stay behind and make sure the tracks are erased," said Josh.

"That is good. These hunters do not have much knowledge of forest, they will need to be taught. While you are in cave, teach them about ways of forest," Tobahana replied. "Let us be on our way."

They reached the stream just before daybreak. Tobahana insisted they wait until sunrise so the men could see where they were walking. He wanted to make sure that no tracks were visible on the way upstream. With Josh lagging behind to cover any inadvertent sign, he was confident they could make it to the cave.

As daylight broke over the mountains, Tobahana watched as Josh and the men waded into the icy cold stream to begin their journey to its origin. At first, no one complained of the icy water, but as each one started upstream, he could hear the grumbling. The only one who did not complain was the old scout, who said the water felt good on his blackened feet.

He waited until they were gone before he began his task of deceiving the Shawnee warriors that were surely on their trail already. The first thing he did was make some tracks on the other side of the stream, which would cause the trackers to wonder as to which way the hunters had gone. Then he came back to the creek and started downstream, leaving a track or overturned stone for them to find. His objective was to get them to follow him downstream, instead of going upstream, where they would find the hunters.

Hoping the deception would work, Tobahana waded down the stream several miles from where he left Josh and the others. He left enough sign that could be found by an experienced tracker, without being too obvious. Staying in the stream, he continued until he reached the junction of a small creek coming from a small valley to his right. Without leaving any tracks, Tobahana made his way up the small tributary, stepping from one small pool to another, as he put more distance between himself and the trackers.

If the Shawnees took the bait, they were probably already on his deceptive trail. He had no way to know if they did, but he couldn't take a chance on going back to check. When he had gone to the end of the creek where it trickled out of a fresh water spring, Tobahana climbed a ridge and found the old tracks he'd left two days ago, as he left the village to get Tana-qate.

He continued to follow the old tracks that led him back to the ridge where he found the cave entrance. Careful not to leave sign on the rocky outcroppings, he found the overhang and dropped over the side to the opening of the cavern. He sat under the overhang for several hours, waiting to see if he had been followed. After hearing no one, Tobahana slipped into the cavern.

Josh and the hunters were just making their way into the large room of the cave. Tobahana was glad to see that they had made it through the bowels of the mountain. He advised them to find a resting place in the cave and continue to be silent for the next few hours, in case the Shawnees were near. So far, they had evaded the war party.

They spent the whole day in silence as the Shawnees scoured the countryside for their trail. As darkness loomed over the forest, Tobahana told the men to share what food they had in their packs. He and Josh still had much of the food Meriah prepared, including dried venison, fruit and vegetables, which the others graciously accepted.

Old Boggs, who still looked as if he might drop over from starvation, was thankful for the food. He chewed on the dried deer meat, savoring it like it was the finest food he'd ever put into his mouth. Tobahana told him to take care and not overstuff or he would be sick and not able to travel when the time came.

Toward nightfall, Josh and Tobahana ventured outside to see if there were signs of the Shawnee war party. They climbed the overhang and scouted along the crest of the mountain, jumping from one outcrop of stone to another, making sure they didn't give their hiding position away. An hour passed before they were satisfied they had not been discovered. However, they couldn't take a chance on leaving the cave, and told the others they should wait for a day or so before resuming their journey south.

Tobahana wanted to go back to the village to see if he could free Timar, but he knew it would only endanger the rescued men. He would return for him when he got them safely out of Shawnee territory. He knew they would have extra guards on Timar until they were sure he wasn't in the area, so it would be up to Timar to stay alive until he could rescue him.

During the second day in the cave, Josh and Tobahana decided it was safe to light a small fire to cook a warm meal. In the far corner of the cave, Josh built a fire from dry wood gathered from under the overhang. The hunters gathered around the small fire to warm themselves, as Tobahana collected cupfuls of snow from near the cave entrance.

When the cups of water were boiling, Josh added dried vegetables and meat from his pack. Soon, they had three cups of hot stew, which were shared by everyone.

Afterwards, by the light of the small fire, Tobahana showed them the strange animal paintings on the wall of the cave. They were amazed to see the paintings of unknown species of animals which must have roamed the countryside at some time in the past. No one could explain the weird-looking beasts, which adorned the wall, but Josh said he'd seen animals that looked similar to the large tusked one, on his travels to India as a sailor in King George's navy. He said they were called elephants, without such long tusks as depicted on the cave wall. They all agreed that many years ago, this part of Kentuckee was a place of many strange animals.

Early on the third day, Tobahana told them it was time to leave the cave and head south. He had scouted the area during the previous night, found no sign of the Shawnees and decided it was safe to resume their trek. The hunters gathered their belongings and followed Tobahana, Josh and Sequah outside to find, to their good fortune, it was starting to snow again. The new snow would cover their tracks and give them an excellent opportunity to get out of Kentuckee without being discovered.

Josh and Tobahana took the lead, striking out in a southerly direction, with the others following single file. Sequah agreed to bring up the rear and kept a sharp eye on their back trail in case the Shawnees picked up their tracks. If the snow continued to fall, it was doubtful any sign would be left for them to find.

When they reached the Big Sandy River next afternoon, they were surprised to find white men camping. Josh approached the camp with caution and called out to the camp before making himself visible to them.

"Hello the camp," he shouted and waited for a response. "I'm Josh Mosby from Virginia."

"Step out so we can see you," came a voice from the camp.

With his rifle cradled in his arms, Josh stepped out of the forest and walked slowly toward the camp. He noticed that there were only three men in the camp and wondered at their boldness for having a blazing fire going, right here in the middle of Shawnee territory.

"They must be unaware of the danger," he thought, as he neared the glowing fire.

Two of the strangers stepped out to greet him. Both were large men, dressed in buckskins, with their rifles held in the firing position. When they could see that Josh was a white man, they lowered their rifles and invited him to join them. He entered the camp and introduced himself.

"Name's Josh Mosby," he repeated, and leaned his rifle against a nearby tree. "My friends and I are on our way home with some hunters that were taken by the Shawnees."

"Did you say hunters who were captured by the Shawnees?" said one of the campers.

"Yes, that's what I said. We've been on the trail for almost a fortnight, trying to arrange their freedom from Chief Black Fish of the Wolf River Shawnees," replied Josh.

"You don't say!" returned the taller of the three. "My brother was taken by the Shawnees near a month past. We got word a week ago by one of the men who was with him. Name was Jim Monay, who said an Indian and a white man were going to look for the captives. Might ye be that white man?"

"I met Monay. Told him we might look for your brother and the others. If your name is Boon, then we have your brother with us," said Josh.

"Name's Squire Boon," said the big man, extending his hand to Josh. "Reckon I owe you a debt of gratitude for what you've done."

Josh called out from the camp and told the others to come on in. In a few minutes, they were greeted with handshakes and welcomed into the camp. Daniel Boon was glad to see his brother and was soon engrossed in a private conversation with him. Young Kenton was slapped on the back by one of the other men, when he heard about his run through the Shawnee gauntlet. Old Boggs sat at the fire and ate at the meat on the spit. Finley introduced Tobahana and Sequah to the others and told them of the sacrifice that Tobahana's brother had made.

Afterwards, they all shared a meal at the fire and Josh reminded them that they were still in hostile Shawnee country, so they extinguished the fire. They all made camp on the Big Sandy that night, but Josh and Tobahana slipped into the forest to stand watch, in case they were visited by the Shawnees.

Chapter Twenty
Timar Faces Death

For the first few hours, they had no mercy on the young Seneca, who had bravely fought the surrounding mob of Shawnee warriors when he was captured. Beaten within an inch of his life, he was dragged back to the village and tied to the post in the clearing. Here, he was pelted with stones, mocked and spit upon by the whole village population. He was still breathing when they finally relented and left him alone to face the freezing night.

Timar drifted in and out of consciousness, but managed to stay alive by moving his feet and legs to keep the blood circulating. His teeth chattered from the cold and he was thankful they hadn't stripped him of his clothing. He felt alone, and dreaded the coming day, knowing that more punishment awaited him.

Before morning light, he was taken to the same room where the hunters had been held and was left alone to ponder his next round of torture. His wounds, though superficial, caused his entire body to ache constantly. Thankful to still be alive, he found the strength to get himself into a sitting position, where he checked the bleeding in several cuts on his head and face. Managing to remove his outer garment, Timar used his flannel under shirt to wipe the blood from his eyes and mouth. From a gourd of water left there by the hunters, he soaked the shirt and cleaned the wounds. When he was satisfied that he could do no more, he put the clothing back on and sat waiting in the corner of the room.

Over and over, he thought of the carelessness of his actions in the exchange of Tana-qate. He should have been more aware of the craftiness of the Shawnee chief's son. One lesson he learned from the incident was to never trust anyone but those of his own family. He resigned himself never to be caught unawares again, if he got out of this situation alive.

Late in the afternoon, two Shawnee maidens came to the room with food and a gourd of fresh water. They lingered until

Timar ate from the bowl and drank from the gourd. Then they brought in herbal medicine and clean bandages to dress his head wounds. He was grateful for their assistance and smiled his appreciation when they left.

At noon on the second day, as a prisoner of the Shawnees, Black Fish came to visit Timar.

"You are brother of Tobahana?" he asked.

"Tobahana of the Senecas is my brother," replied Timar.

"Why does this brother of Tobahana dress like the white man?" he asked again.

"I have lived with my brother-in-law, Josh Mosby for nearly ten years, near the sacred Painted Mountain, far south of here. Only the Cherokees have been our friends and do not mind that I dress as the white man," said Timar.

"The Cherokee people are becoming more and more friendly to the whites who settle on their land. One day, they will realize that the white man will take everything. That is why the Shawnees forbid the longhunters from coming into Kentuckee. If we let them hunt, they will soon move their families and take over the Shawnee lands," said Black Fish.

"It is true that many settlers are coming west each year. There must be a way for them to live peacefully among the Indian nations. Most of them are good people who have left everything to come over the blue mountains to find farmland and raise their families," said Timar.

"Bah! You talk like a white man," spat Black Fish. "They will not be allowed in Shawnee lands. If they enter, they will be dealt with very harshly."

"It is your land," said Timar. "I only know what is happening south of here, in Cherokee lands."

"The Cherokees are weak. They do not see the real danger which comes from the white man. One day, they will see that they do not own the land given to them by the Great Spirit many years ago. They will soon be pushed further and further until there is no place for them to raise their own families." said Black Fish.

Timar decided not to talk more about the white settlers and changed the subject.

"Why has Chief Black Fish come to visit?" asked Timar, knowing that the chief had other plans for him.

"You will see," he said. "It is the custom of our people to require prisoners to prove whether they deserve the friendship of the Shawnee. You will be put before the gauntlet tomorrow at midday. It will prove to my people whether you are worthy to live or die."

When he finished speaking, Black Fish left the room and walked back to his quarters.

Timar was left to ponder the upcoming ordeal that awaited him. He had heard of the Shawnee's murderous gauntlet from his two Cherokee friends, Sequah and Menah, who heard it from Cherokee warriors that had experienced the trial. They told him it was the one thing they feared if ever captured by the Shawnees. Still, he knew others had passed the test. Tobahana recently told him that Simon Kenton, one of the rescued hunters, had gone the distance and lived through the ordeal.

Timar was a strong lad, but with the beating he received only yesterday, he needed time to recover. His head roared with pain from a thousand blows, and every muscle in his body ached as if it were one constant sore. If only he had more time to get his body back to normal. In less than twelve hours, he would meet death in the faces of forty strong, Shawnee warriors who would have no pity on him.

The two maidens brought his evening meal just before sunset. He was glad to receive the nourishment and thanked them for the corn mush and gourd of water. After they departed, he was surprised by another visitor, who slipped through the door like a shadow and stood on the opposite side of the room.

He watched intently, recognizing the figure as another Shawnee maiden. From where he sat in the corner, he could tell she was studying this Seneca, who was now prisoner of the Shawnee people. He waited for several minutes before he spoke in the Iroquois language.

"I am called Timar, brother of Tobahana of the Senecas. I am also brother-in-law of the great white longknife, Josh Mosby, who is married to my sister, Meriah," he said quietly and waited on a response.

She stood against the wall, wrapped in a long cloak with the hood pulled overhead, concealing her face. He could see that she was young, perhaps in her teen years by the shape of her tiny feet adorned with white beaded moccasins. Still, she said not a word, but watched him intently for several minutes. Then, as quietly as she had entered, she glided to the door and was gone.

Timar was puzzled by the strange visitor. Who was she and why hadn't she spoken? Was she there just to check on his condition? Whatever the reason, it took his mind off the event facing him and he spent the better part of the evening pondering over his visitor.

Morning came with a number of Shawnee women entering the room to clean and dress his wounds. He wondered why they hadn't done it when they put him in the room, then he guessed his strange visitor might have something to do with it. After carrying in several basins of water, they made him strip so they could get to the cuts and bruises which covered most of his body. He was ashamed to show his nakedness, but they insisted until he met their demands.

When the women finished bathing Timar, one of them applied a salve consisting of herbs and bear grease to the cuts on his face and head. It made him feel much better, although he probably looked frightful with the putrid colored splotches of the concoction covering most of his face. After they quietly departed, he dressed and waited on the noon hour to come.

Shortly before noon, the hooded Shawnee girl stepped into the room and stood silently against the wall opposite him. For some reason, he was glad that she had not been one of the women who cleaned him up. He could tell she was looking at him, although he could not see her face for the hood she drew tightly over her head.

Once again, he repeated who he was, but she seemed not to acknowledge what he said and remained silent. He wanted to approach closer so he could at least see her face, but decided to let her make the next move. In a few minutes, the hooded figure slipped quietly out the door.

Perplexed over what had just happened, Timar was becoming more interested in the hooded girl than what he was about to face in less than an hour. He could not even guess why she had visited him. Maybe she was the chief's spy to see if he was fit to run the gauntlet. Gauntlet! Suddenly, he realized it was almost time to face the two lines of fierce Shawnee warriors.

He hoped that he would be brave enough to make it through the gauntlet. Were it not for his bruises and sore head, he felt like he could withstand the torturous run, but he was not sure he could do it today. He wished Black Fish had allowed him a few more days to recuperate.

Two large Shawnee braves came for him and led him out of the room. With one on either side of him, they walked toward the center of the village where the gaultlet was already in place. He could see the two lines of fierce-looking warriors as they waved their clubs and switches in the air, shouting obscenities at the approaching Seneca. Suddenly, the drumming started. He thought of it as his own death march as they drew nearer to the gauntlet lines.

Timar dreaded the thought of facing the gauntlet. He knew if he didn't make it through the ordeal, he would never see his family again. His mind was going through a flurry of thoughts, trying to recall why he'd gotten himself into such a mess. If only he had listened to Josh and Meriah.

He looked over the crowd gathered to witness the event, seeing old men, women and a few children, who were shouting threats and curses at him. At the other end of the two lines, stood Black Fish, dressed in his long buffalo robe, with arms folded. Standing beside the chief was the hooded girl. Standing at the chief's other side was Tana-qate.

In the daylight, he could finally see her face. He was not close enough to see very clearly, but what he saw was the most beautiful face he'd ever seen. She was not having any part of the shouting and jeering, looking straight at him with a solemn face, as he approached the head of the lines. If I make it through this mess, I will find out who she is, he thought.

At the end of the gauntlet, the two braves stripped Timar of his shirt and led him forward to the starting point. The drums ceased as Black Fish raised his arm into the air. He spoke loud enough for the crowd to hear.

"This Seneca will now face Shawnee justice for what he has done. He has been party to the capture and mistreatment of my son, Tana-qate. The time has come for his punishment," shouted Black Fish.

Before he could continue, the crowd roared with shouts for the death of the Seneca. It went on for several minutes before Black Fish quieted them.

"As it is the custom of our people, this Seneca deserves to be tested according to the laws set forth by the elders of this village. If he still lives after facing our finest warriors, he will be allowed to keep his life," said Black Fish. "He will not be allowed to leave this village. If he tries to escape, he will caught and put to death."

Timar heard him loud and clear. It looked as if he were doomed to be a prisoner of the Shawnees, whether he lived through the gauntlet or not. One thing he remembered from Tobahana, who had also been a prisoner of the Shawnees: "Never give up hope," he told him. "Sometimes that is all a man has to get him through desperate situations."

Black Fish lowered his arm and the two braves shoved Timar forward. He stumbled as the first warrior hit him in on the side of the head. It was not a hard blow, but it felt as if his head would explode. He shook his head to clear his brain, as a series of hard clubbings hit him on the back, bringing him to his knees. Keen willow switches slashed long weltering cuts across his shoulders and back as he rose to a standing position.

"Run," he thought, trying to clear his head. He bent forward amid the pounding on the back of his head and shoulders and pushed forward. He tried to run, but was stopped by the club of a huge Shawnee brave who hit him squarely in the chest, knocking the wind from his lungs. Timar gasped for air and lowered his head again. This time, he made it halfway through the lines.

With a burst of energy that came from deep inside, he pushed himself further down the gauntlet. Blow upon blow came down as he tried to cover his face with his arms. Blood spurted from his nose and a hundred other places on his tortured body. His eyes burned from blood running down from the cuts on his forehead and he tried to wipe them, only to receive more cutting slashes from the willow-wielding warriors.

Once again, he was brought to his knees by a mighty crash of Shawnee clubs. This time, he thought it was all over. He could feel the consciousness start to fade from his head, when he heard a small voice shouting for him to get up. Somehow, he mustered enough energy to stand and push forward.

He didn't know when he reached the end of the gauntlet. The last thing he saw as he fell forward, was the small figure in the hooded cloak waving him onward.

Chapter Twenty-One
Fight for Survival

Josh and Tobahana awakened the hunters at first light with a warm breakfast of deer stew which they poured into the hunters' cups. They had taken liberty of using Squire Boon's pewter cooking pot to fix it. There was more than enough to go around, even with old Boggs having seconds.

"What is the plan?" asked the older of the Boon brothers.

"Our plan is to go back the way we came to get these men out of Shawnee country safely," said Josh. "If we stay here any longer, we can expect a war party to catch up with us. We need to be on our way as soon as possible."

"Squire and I are not leaving with you," said Daniel. "We had a long talk last night and decided to ride the winter out here in Kentuckee. Ye all know how plentiful the game is here and we're not going back until we've got all we can carry out of here."

"I wouldn't advise it," said Josh Mosby. "The Shawnees will surely find you and you won't be as fortunate next time."

Squire Boon spoke up, "Dan'l tells me that the whole country is teeming with buffalo, elk, beaver, and whitetails. It seems a shame to come this far and not be able to take some of it home with us."

"I doubt if you will. The Shawnee are very adamant about keeping the whites out of Kentuckee. You saw what happened. Look at young Kenton. He almost lost his life because he was with you hunters. Next time, the Shawnees will not be so lenient," replied Josh.

"Ye make it sound worse than we believe it is," said Daniel. "We plan to hunt much farther to the west of Wolf River. Them Shawnees will never know we're in Kentuckee."

"Suit yourself. I only know what other hunters have faced. Those who were fortunate enough to make it back, have said they will never risk hunting in Kentuckee again," said Josh.

Tobahana, who was listening to their conversation, decided to interject a coment. "You are fortunate to be freed from the Shawnee. Why do you risk going back to face their savage treatment?"

Boon answered, "I want to thank ye for your trouble in rescuing us. I know the lad who was captured was yer brother and I shore feel sorry to see him in the hands of Black Fish."

He went on the explain why he was going to stay in Kentuckee. "Me and my brother, Squire, have talked it over and decided that since we're both here, we're going to try to last out the winter. It would take us two or three years to get outfitted for another trip and by then, there will be hundreds of hunters and settlers coming into Kentuckee. We want to be able to see the country and stake our claim on some of this land, if it ever comes available."

"I can understand how you feel about the land. But you must realize that Black Fish and his Wolf River Shawnees are not the only Indians in the territory. Several other tribes will fight to keep their land," replied Josh. "There's the Mingos, Illinois, and Miami, who also protect these hunting grounds. I'm afraid you fellers will have more trouble than you realize."

"Well, we're gonna give it a go," said Boon. "Reckon ye could take these boys on back to Virginia?"

"We can do that," said Josh. "We'll probably need their help before we get out of Shawnee country."

Daniel and Squire said their goodbyes and watched the group of hunters gather their packs for the trip out of Kentuckee. The two men who accompanied Squire Boon decided the danger was too great to stay and joined the departing men. Josh and Tobahana thought it was better to go back the same route, following the river through the great canyon near the border of Virginia. John Finley agreed.

There were seven in all: Josh, Tobahana, Sequah, John Finley, Simon Kenton and the two new men, John Riley and Jim Conley. They departed the Boon brothers before noon, traveling along the south side of the river.

A day later found them at the entrance to the wild mountain gorge where they had captured the Shawnee lad, Tana-qate. Tobahana decided to call a halt and camp in the forest near the river, while he scouted the gorge for Shawnee sign. The gorge was a perfect place for an ambush and Tobahana knew it would be the most likely place for the Shawnees to attack them.

He crossed the river and climbed the high peak of the ridge where he and Josh traveled with their prisoner. He was careful not to leave any sign, knowing it was a well-used trail. When he reached the rim of the gorge and peered down, he could see the stream coursing its way like a ribbon far below. Directly across from where he lay on the high rock cliff, a towering spire rose from the stream level, like a primitive castle reaching into the evening sky. Upstream from there, he recognized the small opening on the mountainside where he and Josh left the first Shawnees they encountered.

Tobahana studied the panorama of the area for any sign of movement. The only thing he saw moving were the eagles as they soared around the tall castle-like tower in front of him. He watched as one of them glided down through the wide gorge to take a trout from the stream below and returned to its perch in a tall pine tree growing on the tower.

After an hour of watching, Tobahana was satisfied that there were no Shawnees in the area and decided it was safe to pass through the gorge. He took his time returning to the camp. Along the way, he noticed many deer trails and even spotted one huge whitetail buck as it watched him move stealthily along the crest of the mountain. Were it not for the danger of Shawnees hearing the gunshot, they would have had fresh venison for the evening meal.

Just before dusk, Tobahana returned to the camp where he found everyone in good spirits. They were discussing the good fortune of having been rescued from the Shawnees. The two new men were all ears and old Boggs was laying it on thick. When he showed them his blackened feet with a few toes missing, they were astonished that the Indians would do that to a man.

Tobahana told them he found no Shawnee sign and it looked like the area was clear. They would be following the stream through the gorge at first light. He told them they were only two days from the farm of Josh Mosby and would be safe to return to their families from there. The men were glad to hear that their problems were almost over.

After a cold night without a fire, morning came with a thick frost that covered everything in sight. All around, the trees looked like huge, white ghostly specters, bowing to welcome them to a day of unknown adventure. The hunters grumbled at the cold breakfast of dried deer meat and water from the stream, but soon were packed up and ready to begin the last leg of their journey to freedom.

Tobahana and Josh moved out first, cautiously scouting ahead of the others. They had no way to disguise their footprints in the heavy frost, hoping the sun would take care of them later in the morning. The stones along the stream bed were slick and dangerous to walk on; however it was the only way to get through the gorge. The hunters were warned to take caution. They couldn't afford to waste time because of a broken leg as the result of a fall on the stones.

Josh heard it first! It sounded like a small stone careening off the side of the gorge wall somewhere up ahead. He stopped to warn Tobahana, who was climbing over a boulder a few yards behind him. As he turned, a splatter of lead burst into the boulder, followed by the echo of a gunshot, which reverberated down the gorge. Josh jumped backward and took cover with Tobahana behind the boulder.

"Shawnees!" said Tobahana. "Must have slipped into the gorge after darkness came last night."

"What do we do now?" came Josh's question.

"We must get back and warn the others to take cover. You go and I will see how many Shawnee are up ahead," said Tobahana. "Keep your head down."

Josh was about to leap over the boulder behind them when a hail of gunfire greeted them from the rim of the gorge. Rifle balls ricochetted off the rocks, others sent water splashing from the stream nearby, followed by the loud staccato of gunshots echoing through the crisp morning air. White puffs of smoke rose from places all along the rim, giving the location of the Shawnee war party. Josh and Tobahana were pinned down with no place to go.

"Looks like a big party from the looks of that smoke," said Josh as he peered over the boulder and looked up at the rim several hundred yards above them.

"Shawnee not very accurate from that distance," replied Tobahana. "Too far. They will try to keep us here while they send warriors to attack hunters and Sequah."

"Then, we must risk going back to warn them," said Josh.

Another round of gunfire boomed from high on top of the gorge, causing them to take cover again.

"If we make a run for it while they're reloading, I think we can get out of range of their guns," said Josh.

"I think it is our only chance to save others," replied Tobahana. When next round comes, we will run."

After the next fusillade of lead balls rained down from the heights, both of them scrambled from behind their sheltering boulder and ran as fast as they could. Two or three shots sounded as the Shawnees tried to hit the fleeing pair, but the distance was too far and the bullets fell short. Josh and Tobahana leapt over large stones and sped down the gorge, putting the shooters farther and farther behind them. Before they exited the gorge, they heard nothing from the top of the gorge.

"Looks like we outran their ambush," said Josh, stopping for a second to catch his breath.

"We have not seen last of Shawnee warriors," replied Tobahana. "They will follow along top of gorge and try again."

"We had better hurry and warn the others, so we can get ready for their attack," said Josh.

The hunters were glad to see them return. They had heard

the gunfire as it echoed through the gorge and were worried that Josh and Tobahana might not make it back. Some of the hunters were anxious to get into battle with the Shawnees, but Tobahana told them the timing was not right for a confrontation. It would come later, when the Shawnees were ready.

"Shawnees will send war party to attack us from rear," said Tobahana. "They will try to surround us. We must get prepared to meet them."

"What would you have us do?" asked Finley.

"We have very short time to get ready. Must make stone walls for protection," he said, pointing to the stones along the stream.

Soon, every man was carrying river stones and placing them onto three hastily constructed walls. The walls were not very high, but would suffice in giving them some protection against the Shawnee rifle balls and arrows that were sure to come. When the small fortification was completed, they gathered all their supplies inside and waited for the coming fight.

"We are at a terrible disadvantage," said Josh. "They command the heights, so be very careful about giving them a target."

Two men were put at each of the walls where they could watch for the advance of the Shawnees. Tobahana, who stood alone in the center of the fort, acted as lookout and watched all four directions for sign of the war party. Each man was armed with longrifle, knife and a good supply of lead shot and powder. In addition, Josh, Tobahana and Sequah carried tomahawks and flintlock pistols tucked into their belts.

As the day wore on, they waited for the upcoming battle, hoping that the Shawnees would attack them at their small fort where there was protection. Tobahana told them the Shawnees would wait until they figured the white men were growing tired and complacent, then hit them with a quick attack. They would carry the battle to them on Shawnee terms, and they must be ready when that time came.

An hour after the sun had reached the southern rim of the gorge, the Shawnees made their first attempt, sending a dozen wild, yelling braves toward the stone fortification. Tobahana saw them first, as the war party emerged from the trees a hundred yards downstream. They rushed forward with rifles and tomahawks waving wildly in the air.

Josh Mosby fired first. The forward brave stopped dead in his tracks, taking a rifle ball squarely in the chest. The others rushed on as Tobahana and the hunters fired into the charging braves. Three more went down, crashing into the stony bank of the stream. The rest of the Shawnees dove for cover, hiding among the rocks and boulders some fifty yards away.

The hunters yelled loudly, having stopped the attack, but Tobahana cautioned them to be ready for the next charge. Quickly reloading their longrifles, they calmed down and waited. The wait wasn't long; twenty or more warriors burst out of the trees and ran straight toward the little fort.

Tobahana shouted for four of the hunters to fire. Old Boggs, Finley, and the two new men fired at once, taking two of the rushing warriors out of the battle. After firing, they dropped down and began to reload as Tobahana, Josh and the others released a hail of bullets toward the attackers. Surprised at the accuracy of the longrifles, the war party wavered in disarray and took cover in the rocks near the first group of warriors.

Josh laid his rifle over the stone wall and waited for the first head to appear some fifty yards away. It wasn't long before two black-faced Shawnees raised up and looked toward the little fort of hunters. Josh centered his sights on the brave on the right and fired, sending a rifle ball into his forehead. The other brave yelled some obscenity and dove for cover.

Things settled down for a few minutes, while the Shawnees planned their next move. During the lull, Tobahana told the others to prepare for a rush at their position. The war party would be coming straight for them and would not stop unless they were hit by a rifle ball. The ones who were not hit would be over the fortification with war clubs and tomahawks, and would try to kill everyone.

Behind the stone walls, each of the men made sure their

rifles were loaded and their knives handy. They would have only one shot before the attackers reached them. Then it would be a hand-to-hand fight for survival. Josh, Tobahana, and Sequah checked their pistols and kept their tomahawks where they could reach them.

Young Kenton was anxious to get his revenge for the terrible treatment he received while captured. He was now stronger, having regained most of his strength. The trek from the Shawnee village had given him a chance to test his legs and arms and he refused to let any of the others carry his pack. Keeping his rifle in firing position, he peered over the stone wall and waited for the war party to resume their attack. He actually looked forward to the Shawnees' next move.

Tobahana was concerned about the hunters. They had never faced such savage warriors in close combat and he was worried that they might not be able to fend off another attack. He told them to wait until they were sure of their target before firing. Every shot had to count, even then, they might not stop the Shawnees. They would be coming over the wall with all the strength they could muster.

Young Kenton saw them break from their hiding position in the rocks and yelled the warning. The savages were coming fast, jumping from boulder to boulder, heading directly toward the small fort. Tobahana told them to hold their fire until the Shawnees were within a dozen yards of the wall.

At his signal, everyone fired at the same time. White smoke from the flintlocks filled the air, making it impossible to see how many of the war party were down. Each man dropped his rifle, drew his knife and waited for the assault over the wall. They came out of the haze of white smoke, nearly a dozen black-faced, screaming warriors swinging war clubs and tomahawks, and were over the wall in an instant.

Tobahana and Josh fired their pistols, taking two of the savages down before they had a chance to wield their clubs. The hunters proved to be worthy, as they engaged the Shawnee warriors. Of the dozen braves who were now inside the small fort, only one was able to inflict a damaging blow. He managed to plunge his tomahawk into the back of the new man, John Riley, who went down, unable to rise from the blow. Tobahana, who was engaged hand-to-hand with a strong warrior, saw him go down and feared the worst for Riley.

Josh and Tobahana stood back to back and fended off the attackers with knife and tomahawk. They hacked and plunged away at the savages, sending three more to the spirit world, while the hunters were also getting the best of the enemy. It lasted only five minutes or less with the last of the Shawnees scrambling back over the wall. Old Boggs, who had reloaded his rifle, waited until the brave reached a hundred yards and sent a ball between his shoulder blades.

They were fortunate to have lost only one man. Several of them had cuts and scrapes, but no serious wounds. They congratulated each other on their victory. Tobahana said the Shawnees would try again, but would wait until another day. They'd had enough this day.

They took the time to bury John Riley before leaving their little fort. On the stream bank, they dug a shallow grave and heaped river stones on it, hoping the wild animals would not bother the body. Then, Tobahana led the group upstream, hoping to get through the gorge before the Shawnees attacked again.

Darkness came as they reached the site of the cave where Josh and Tobahana left the two dead Shawnee braves. He decided they should stay in the small cave until morning light before traversing the dangerous last leg of the gorge. They found the bodies of the Shawnees just where they had been placed. The cold weather kept their bodies from deteriorating and they carried stones to cover them at the rear of the cave.

Josh and Tobahana stood watch at the entrance of the cavern while the others managed to catch a few hours of sleep. There had been no supper meal, only a few bites of dried deer meat, which they gnawed until it was soft enough to swallow.

Chapter Twenty-Two
Timar's Dilemma

Timar didn't regain consciousness until the next day. The last warrior in the line hit him on the back of the head, knocking him out as he reached the end of the gauntlet. He couldn't remember making it through, only that someone had called his name at the last moment.

When he awoke, he found that he had been moved into a Shawnee living quarter where several women were busy attending to him. He had been bathed and medicine applied to his wounds. His head still throbbed from the beating and the cuts stung from the salty salve they'd rubbed into them. Other than that, Timar was glad to still be among the living.

He spent three days under the care of the Shawnee nurses. They were courteous and saw to his needs, watching his wounds for infection, and seeing that he had ample food to eat. He was getting his strength back and could feel his wounds beginning to heal. The thing that bothered him was being unsure of what lay ahead; whether he was to receive more punishment, or even death at the stake. Whatever happened, Timar assured himself of facing it like a Seneca warrior.

At the end of the third day, his mysterious visitor returned. This time, she was not wearing the hooded cloak. She was dressed in a beautiful tan doeskin dress, decorated with trade beads and dyed porcupine quills, her small feet adorned with matching doeskin moccasins.

She wore her shiny black hair in two long braids which streamed over her shoulders and rested on her breasts. Around her head was a band of white cloth, decorated with beautiful lapis lazuli beads. The large brown eyes accenting her small beautiful face could see that he was interested in finding out who she was.

She took a seat near Timar's bed and quietly spoke in the

Iroquois language. "I am called Telah, daughter of the great chief of the Wolf River Shawnees. I am glad to see you are recovering from the run through the warriors."

"Glad to meet you, Telah," said Timar as he raised himself up to a sitting position on the bed of furs. "I saw you standing by your father and heard someone call out my name. Was that someone you?"

"I always take the side of the one who runs the gauntlet. No one else would dare to encourage the enemy of the Shawnees," she replied in answer to his question.

"Your father is a hard man. I can see why no one would go against his wishes," said Timar.

"My father will be coming to visit you soon. He will give you the choice of staying to live here with the Wolf River people, or refusing and receiving more punishment. I hope you decide to live with my people," she said in an almost pleading tone.

"My home is far south of Wolf River. I live with my brother-in-law and my sister on a small farm in the land of the Cherokees. I would miss my family if I stayed here.

"You will not have the opportunity to go home. My father has already decided not to set you free. You have heard the choices. He will hold you to them," said Telah.

He watched her as she rose from her seat and started toward the doorway. Her lithe figure turned and she said one last statement before leaving. "You will give it much thought and I hope you make the wise choice."

Timar already knew he didn't want to face another run in the gauntlet or some other form of torture by the Shawnees. At least, he was alive and recuperating. He remembered the words of his brother, Tobahana, who said, "A man always has hope as long as he lives."

Black Fish came to see him early next morning just as Telah had said. He laid out his demands first, telling Timar he was welcome to live with his people, but would be required to take an oath, swearing allegiance to the Wolf River Shawnees, and gave him until noon the following day to make the decision.

When Black Fish departed, Timar was left alone in the room to ponder his dilemma. In his condition, he knew he had no chance to escape. Tobahana and Josh were now out of the picture and he knew they were obligated to get the hostages out of Shawnee territory. His options were very slim, leaving him with the only one feasible alternative and that was to do as Black Fish had requested.

Well, he knew he had at least one friend in the village. That is, if she was as sincere as she seemed to be. He wanted to get to know her better and looked forward to her next visit. Timar didn't know why she'd taken an interest in him, especially since he was an outsider. Maybe she was trying to defy her father for some reason.

She came again in the late afternoon, bringing his evening meal, which she had prepared for him. It consisted of a bowl of warm venison stew containing several kinds of vegetables, along with several baked corn cakes. He was glad to have something different than the bowl of corn mush and water they were feeding him. She sat and watched him eat, noting his approval by quickly devouring every bite of the tasty stew.

"You must have been hungry," she said, when he had finished eating.

"Thank you," he replied. "It was one of the best meals I've ever eaten."

He sat on the side of the bed and watched his host as she placed the empty bowl and spoon into the basket. Timar wanted to learn more about her, but was a little shy, being in the presence of such a beautiful woman. He started to ask about her family, but knew it would be improper to ask personal questions, so he waited for her to speak first.

Before leaving, she said, "You will be adopted into one of the families here in the village. That is, if you decide to stay with us."

Timar didn't understand what she meant by being adopted into a Shawnee family and asked her to explain.

"It is the custom of our people to adopt those who choose to live among us. It means that you will live in the quarters of one of our families and they will treat you as an adopted son. You will be given the freedom to go anywhere within the village, as long as you obey the rules. You must never go outside the village without someone with you," she declared.

He listened as she continued.

"When you have gained the trust of our people, you will be allowed outside the village to hunt or visit other villages. At first, you will hunt with other warriors who will try your allegiance to the Shawnee people. After time passes, when you have proven yourself to them, they will allow you the same freedom as all warriors have."

"I guess I have no other choice but to be adopted," said Timar.

"It would be better than dying," she replied. "It is far better to live among our people than lose your life in the run through the warriors. My father has given me permission to teach you the ways of the Shawnee. He will expect results when he visits you tomorrow at noontime. Please do not let me disappoint him."

She rose to leave but Timar stopped her by asking another question. "When will you teach me about your people? There is not much time left before your father comes for my answer."

"I will return before the sun rises tomorrow. We will have six hours to talk before my father returns," she said.

She left the room quickly, leaving Timar to think about his upcoming adoption into the Shawnee village.

What would Tobahana do in a spot like this, he thought. And what will Meriah say when they get home without him. He promised her he would be with them, but that would not happen, now.

Timar lay awake most of the night. His mind flashed a thousand thoughts about his immediate future and the problems he would be facing. How would he be able to adapt to the Shawnee way of life, since he had spent nearly half of his young life living on the farm of Josh Mosby?

He tried to recall the days of his younger life in his homeland of the Senecas on the Ontario Lake. He remembered being taken hostage by the Shawnees with his sister, Meriah and how they were treated by the Hurons and the disgusting Frenchman, Charboneau, in Montreal. He and Meriah were fortunate to have been rescued by Josh Mosby and Tobahana, but it looked as if he would not be so lucky this time. He was alone and would have to make the best of the situation.

Telah was back before sunup. She brought food with her and they both shared a warm breakfast of corn mush, sweetened with honey. After they'd eaten, she began to teach Timar about the Shawnee way of life.

"My people have been here on Wolf River for many years. My father, Black Fish, was elected chief by the elders of the village soon afterwards and has ruled over our people since. Our village is only one of many small villages south of the Ohio River, in Kentuckee. Most of our people live north of the Ohio, but use the hunting grounds here to supply their winter storehouses," she began to explain.

"My people are not the savages most white men say they are. We live in peace with the other tribes in our area, such as the Mingo, Illinois and Miamis who live north of the big river, but hunt in Kentuckee. However, the Shawnee people will attack anyone who tries to take our game or settle in our land. There have been those of our people who have made bad names for themselves, such as the scarfaced chief who took his braves on the warpath several years ago. We heard that he was killed leading his warriors against the Cherokees. There has been peace among the Shawnee tribes since," said Telah.

"I was once a prisoner of Scarface," said Timar. "He arranged for my sister and me to be captured by the Hurons and kept as hostages by the French. My brother, Tobahana and Josh Mosby rescued us. It is true that he led a battle against the Cherokees. I was there when it happened. Josh Mosby, who married my sister, Meriah, was the one who killed Scarface," replied Timar.

"You must have been very young since it happened nearly ten years ago," said Telah.

"Yes, I was only fourteen summers old and I was not afraid of Scarface. I stood up to him but he was too strong for such a young lad," he replied. "When it was all over, I went to live with my sister and Josh Mosby on his farm in the land of the Cherokees."

"You have seen much in your short lifetime. I have never been able to leave the village on Wolf River. My father watches too closely for me to stray very far," she said. "I have talked with many who have come to our village. They tell of great numbers of white men who come from big cities in the east to settle in Indian lands."

Timar saw the sadness appear in Telah's eyes. He knew she was not happy living here on Wolf River. He could tell that she was interested in hearing about things outside of her confined world. He would tell her about the places and things he'd seen during his lifetime, if she would let him. After facing her father at noon today, he wondered if he would ever get the opportunity to talk with her again.

They sat and talked until it was time for her to leave. He wanted to say much more to her but didn't want to monopolize the conversation. Besides, he liked to hear her voice and was glad she was not too shy to speak to him. He wished the morning could have lasted longer.

Black Fish came promptly at noon. He wasted no time in explaining what was expected of Timar. Since Telah had told him about being adopted, he was not surprised when her father said he would be living with a Shawnee family.

"You will be allowed to keep your name until you have proved your allegiance to our people. When that time comes, you will be given a Shawnee name," he said.

Then, with a stern look directly into Timar's eyes, he said,

"Do not try to escape. You are now the property of our people. You will do whatever your new family asks. If you prove your honor, then you will be treated as one of our people."

Timar felt as if his previous life had just come to an end. He had no alternative but to submit to the demands of his captor, who stood waiting on his decision.

"I will do as you have asked," said Timar.

"Then, you are free to go where you wish as long as it is within the confines of our village. You will be watched at all times. Do not give us cause to put you in confinement again," said the chief. "I will let you know which family you will be living with."

Black Fish left Timar standing in the open doorway with a blank stare on his face. What was he supposed to do now? He was all alone in the middle of the enemy's village knowing only one person by name and she was nowhere to be seen. A complete sense of loneliness came over him as he stood and watched the inhabitants of the village who were going about their daily chores. They didn't even notice the Seneca brave who would soon be a part of them.

Telah walked across the compound with two older Shawnee women and stopped when she reached Timar. She began talking with both of them, pointing to the young man standing in the doorway. When she came closer, she explained to Timar that these women were now his new family.

"This is Tilpa and Mistha. They have recently lost their husbands in battle against the white settlers. You will be staying in their lodge and helping them to get through the winter months. You will be responsible for their welfare, since you are the only male member of their family," Telah explained.

"Whose decision was it to put me in the family of these women?" asked Timar. "

"It was my father's decision. He said you would be able to prove your allegiance to the Shawnee people if you took the responsibility to live with Tilpa and Mistha as their adopted son," she replied with a smile that he didn't quite understand.

"You mean live with them as their son?" he asked.

"That is what I said. You will do as they direct you. You will not be asked to do anything they would not require of their natural son," Telah remarked. "I think you will find that Shawnee women have great respect for their husbands and sons."

Timar suspected there was some kind of hidden message in her statement, but he was not going to argue with her about Black Fish's decision. He would talk to her about it later, if he had a chance.

"I guess I will be living with Tilpa and Mistha. Would you introduce them to their new son?" asked Timar.

Chapter Twenty
End of the Trail

John Finley and his group of hunters were glad to finally get out of the territory of Kentuckee. It had been a long hard trip since he left the Ohio River more than six months ago. As they crossed the final range of mountains and headed down to the Clinche River, he told Tobahana and Josh it would probably be his last foray into Shawnee territory; said he was getting too old to take such strenuous hunting trips and would be staying closer to home from now on.

"I want to thank ye for coming after us," he said to Josh and Tobahana. "Weren't for you two, we'd still be in that mess we got ourselves into back at the winter camp."

"We wouldn't have known about you except for your partners who made it to my farm," said Josh. "We were on our way to Fort Pitt to do some work for the British commandant there. We decided to detour to see if we could give you men a hand."

"You say you were on the way to Fort Pitt?" asked Finley.

"Yes, we have both given the commandant our services in the past," replied Josh. "Seems like he wants us to locate the source of some Indian trouble here on the frontier."

"Maybe it was a good thing you didn't make it to the fort. There has been much trouble between the colonialist and the British. Looks like there might be a war brewing in the east. If it happens, all troops will be pulled out of the western forts and sent back to join with the commander of the British forces in the colonies," said Finley. "That will mean no forces here on the frontier to protect the settlers. I fear that we have not heard the last of Black Fish and marauding Shawnees."

"I guess that might delay our trip to Fort Pitt until we see what will happen," replied Josh. "No use risking the trip till we see if the British abandon Fort Pitt."

"Seems to me, you and Tobahana will have to decide

which side you're going to be on," said Finley. "If the British make war on America, a lot of settlers here on the frontier will be called on to fight on the side of the colonists."

"Guess we'll make that decision when the time comes," said Josh. "Right now, we need to get across the Clinche River and out of Shawnee territory."

Eight weary men crossed the river about twenty miles from the home of Josh Mosby and made camp on the south bank. They risked a fire and cooked what was left of their food supplies. Josh and Tobahana melted into the forest after they'd eaten a bite to stand watch over the camp.

Tomorrow, they would reach Josh's farm and have to face Meriah. Both dreaded to tell her why Timar was not with them. She would not blame them, but herself, for letting him talk her into going. She would never forgive herself.

The last morning on the trail came with a sudden abnormal chill in the air. The hunters huddled around the fire and watched as Sequah prepared breakfast. He was up early and speared several nice smallmouth bass from the Clinche River, which he was now roasting in the fire.

After they devoured the tasty fish, Tobahana told them to pack up for the final twenty miles. The danger of being overtaken by the Shawnees was past, now that they were out of their hunting grounds. It was unlikely to run into the enemy forces on this side of the Clinche. They crossed the last mountain and turned up the little valley toward Josh's home.

Sequah told them he was going to leave them and go on to his Cherokee home, which was sixty miles southwest of them. Josh and Tobahana both thanked him for his help in getting the hunters back, and asked him to spend a few days at the farm. He declined the offer, saying that his family would be worried and he needed to get home. They shook hands and bade farewell to the young Cherokee.

They could see the smoke rising from the little cabin as they crossed the little creek. A warm fire and a hot meal would feel good after being on the trail for nearly a month. Meriah would be glad to see them return unharmed, but they dreaded to tell her the bad news.

Finley said he and the others would be on their way, but Josh insisted they stay until they had time to recuperate from the trip. Besides, he had already told them what a good cook Meriah was, and he wanted to show them his hospitality. After discussing it with the others, Finley and the hunters accepted his offer.

Meriah saw them crossing the creek and ran to meet them. She hugged and kissed Josh, then turned her attention to Tobahana, seeing the sadness in his eyes.

"Where is Timar?" she cried, as she looked over the motley crew with them.

Tobahana was first to speak, saving Josh the problem of explaining Timar's capture.

"Our brother is still living. He was taken prisoner by the Shawnee chief, Black Fish. We were unable to stop them from capturing Timar," Tobahana told her.

"How did it happen? Why were you not able to save him?" she sobbed.

Josh held her tightly to him trying to comfort his beloved wife. He could feel her shaking as she buried her face in his chest and cried.

"We were involved in the exchange of prisoners," said Josh. "By a fortunate turn of events, Tobahana and I were able to capture Chief Black Fish's son. We used the Shawnee boy to bring about the exchange of prisoners. Timar agreed to help, even though we tried to talk him out of it. He stayed in the Shawnee village while Tobahana escorted the hostages to safety. Then he was to walk toward us while we released the chief's son. As they met in the middle of the clearing, Tana-qate, the Shawnee boy, tackled Timar and held him until he was surrounded by the entire force of Shawnee warriors. There was nothing we could do but leave him there. We had to get the white hunters to safety."

"Timar is a strong man," said Josh. "He will survive until we can rescue him."

"Why did it have to happen to Timar? He and I have been through so many terrible tragedies. I fear he will not live through the torture that will be done to him by the Shawnees," she sobbed.

Tobahana tried to make her feel better. "Chief Black Fish is honest. He will not put Timar to death, since we have delivered his only son back to him."

After both had comforted Meriah for several minutes, she was feeling some better and invited everyone to accompany her into the cabin. They accepted and were soon gathered around the big fireplace in the living room of Josh's home. Little Katy was waiting for them and greeted her father and uncle with hugs and kisses. She couldn't wait to show them how much the bear cub had grown.

Tobahana and Josh were pleasantly surprised to see the old man sitting in the kitchen. The old Indian let out a whoop and scrambled to his feet, grabbing both of them at the same time. He shook their hands and slapped them on the back, then stepped back to look at his old friends. Josh and Tobahana were all smiles as old Miskka waited for their response.

"Good to see our old friend," said Tobahana. "You still look same as Cherokee warrior who helped us escape from Frenchman."

"You haven't changed, Miskka," said Josh. "We knew you had come. Timar told us of your visit. I'm glad you waited until we returned."

"It is good to see my old friends," replied the old Cherokee. "I wanted to visit the farm of Josh Mosby before it is too late. Soon, I will be going to the home of my ancestors."

Josh introduced Miskka to the group of hunters and told them of the great service he did in their escape from the Huron and French many years ago. They were impressed with the story and looked at the old Indian with respect. He grinned while Josh related how Miskka still fought the Shawnees while carrying their bullet in his shoulder.

The hunters lingered in the living room until after supper,

when Josh showed them to their sleeping quarters in the shed behind the cabin. They thanked him for his hospitality and said they would be leaving for the east at daybreak.

The three old friends sat near the fireplace and talked about old times. Miskka's eyes were still bright and clear, but his wrinkled face and silvery white hair showed his age. He had long since lost his last tooth and showed his gums when he laughed. Midnight found them still relating their adventures of the time when they were on the trail.

Finley and his party of hunters departed the Mosby farm early next morning. Tobahana and Josh were there to see them off. Meriah gathered enough food to see them back across the blue mountains and they were grateful for her hospitality. They exchanged handshakes and bid their farewells.

Old Boggs expressed his appreciation to them for freeing him from the Shawnees. He said he would still be rotting in their village if they had left him. He vowed never to go back to being a scout and told them if he lived to be a hundred, he'd never venture into Shawnee lands again.

Old Miskka admitted that he was responsible for Meriah agreeing to let Timar go into Kentuckee. He tried to explain his side of the story, but the more he talked, the more trouble he got into with Meriah. She just couldn't get over letting Sequah and Timar talk her into consenting to their trip.

"It is no one's fault," said Josh. "Timar knew the danger. Besides, he and his Cherokee friends have gone on many trips into Kentuckee."

"Yes, my sister," said Tobahana. "Timar knew what he was doing. His part in the exchange of the hostages was very important. They are free because of his willingness to be a part of it. I am certain that he would do it again to save others."

"I just don't understand how he was taken prisoner when you were standing there watching it happen," said Meriah.

"It all happened so fast, we couldn't get to Timar before

he was surrounded by fifty or more Shawnee warriors," said Josh.

"We would have lost our lives and the lives of the hunters if we'd gone back," said Tobahana. "There were too many warriors to fight."

Josh tried to ease the worry which showed on Meriah's face. "Timar will be alright. He is a strong young man and will stand up against anyone who tries to hurt him. We will get him back."

Meriah felt some better hearing Josh's last statement. However, she still blamed herself for him being captured by the Shawnees. Tobahana and Josh assured her that they would be back on the trail as soon as possible.

Old Miskka told them that during his years as a slave to the Shawnees, he was not harmed by the general population of the villages where he had been held. Only one Shawnee had given him any trouble and that was the dreaded Scarface, who had long since met his deserved death. He told Meriah that it was the practice of the Shawnees to adopt outsiders into their tribe, giving them the opportunity to live in peace with them.

"If Timar is as bright as I think he is, he will allow them to adopt him. That will keep him from facing the gauntlet or any other torture. If what I hear Josh and Tobahana say about Black Fish is right, he is a fair man and will give Timar the opportunity to become part of their village," Miskka assured her.

"He is resourceful," said Meriah. "I doubt if he would let them torture him if there was a way he could get out of it."

"Then, he will be alright," said Miskka.

Later, Josh and Tobahana thanked the old Cherokee for easing Meriah's mind about her little brother. He said it was true about the Shawnees adopting people into their tribe, that they even adopted white hostages who would pledge their allegiance to the Shawnee people. It made Josh feel better, but Tobahana could not see his little brother becoming a Shawnee.

"Timar will always be a Seneca," said Tobahana. "He was raised from childhood as a Seneca, and he will never be anyone but a Seneca."

"Even if he agrees to be adopted, he will never forget who he is,' said Josh. "For the present, let's hope that he is given that option. It will keep him alive until we can free him."

Plans for a return trip into Kentuckee were delayed because of old Miskka. Three days after their return home, the old Cherokee fell ill. They suspected a case of pneumonia had befallen their old friend, who had ventured out into the weather to feed the bear cub for little Katy.

He loved her like his own grandaughter and would not allow her outside to feed the animals. It was a responsibility he had taken on himself after Josh and Tobahana left for Kentuckee and he saw no reason to let anyone else do it now. Besides, he wanted to be helpful and it was a job he looked forward to doing.

Josh ordered him to bed and told him not to get out until he recovered from the rattles which plagued his ancient body. Meriah treated him with some of her home remedies, making him swallow a concoction of lamp oil and sugar three times a day, which seemed to ease his breathing. She also put a poultice of mint and other herbs on his chest, saying it would chase away the evil spirits which caused his discomfort.

Old Miskka grew weaker as the days dragged on. His breathing became hoarse and caused him to gasp for air. He tried to tell them it was just a spell of the ague and he would be over it before the week was out.

By the end of the week, Miskka was barely alive. He had grown so weak, he could not raise his head from the pillow. Meriah told Josh and Tobahana that they should speak their last words to their old friend, fearing the end was near.

Josh sat close by the bed and held the hand of the man who meant so much to him. Tobahana stood on the other side of the bed and looked down upon the old Cherokee. Both agreed that time was getting short and expressed their thanks to Miskka for being their faithful friend.

"Miskka, old friend, we have come far since we first met on the French ship many years ago," said Josh. "You have been our friend all these years and we've never forgotten the man who made it possible for us to be here today."

He felt the tremble in the old man's hand as he continued, "Meriah and I gave your name to our daughter, because you meant so much to us. Katherine Miskka Mosby will wear your name proudly for as long as she lives. She has learned to love you as the 'grandfather' she never had. Thank you, old friend for coming to see us one last time."

Tobahana did not know how to express his love for the old Cherokee. He thought of many things he wanted to say, but couldn't put them into words. Instead, he bent low to the ear of the old friend and spoke softly.

"We have come to the end of the trail together, my friend. You will soon be starting on a new journey into the world of the spirits where you will take many new trails with your ancestors. We will all join you on the journey when our time comes," said Tobahana.

Miskka stirred and managed to smile at his friends. "This old Cherokee has come to the end of the trail." He gasped and continued, "You are the reason I have lived for eighty summers. I am glad that I will pass into the spirit world in the home of my friends. I will carry your names with me forever."

Miskka, the old Cherokee passed into the spirit world later that night. Meriah was at his bedside when he breathed his last, and called Josh and Tobahana. They came and stood with her as she covered his face with the sheet.

"He was a good man," she sobbed. "We will miss him."

"I am grateful Miskka was our friend," said Josh.

"I, too, will remember Miskka of the Cherokees," said Tobahana.

They buried him on the hill above the Mosby cabin, near the grave of Josh's first wife, Katherine. Josh read from his worn copy of the Holy Bible as his friends bade their last farewell. Overhead, a flock of geese, with an empty spot in the formation, honked on their way north.

Chapter Twenty-Four
Telah's Story

The wintry days were dragging for Timar, who had now fully recovered from his beating He was not comfortable with his new family that doted over him as if he were their only son. Tilpa and Mistha saw that he was well fed and looked forward to doing things for him. They seemed to be competing for his attention and he didn't know how to divide his time equally between them.

The only bright point of his day was the short time in the afternoons when Telah came by to visit. Telah said she was there to see that he was recuperating, but Timar suspected she wanted to hear him talk of the outside world. Her father made sure that she was followed by one of his trusted braves, who stood at the doorway during her visits.

While Tilpa and Mistha were busy about their chores, Timar would ask Telah personal questions about her father and how she and Tana-qate got along as Black Fish's only children. She was slow to give him any information about her family, not yet trusting him. When she finally began to tell her life's story, Timar was surprised.

"I have never told anyone about my family," said Telah. "You must never repeat what I am about to tell you."

Timar was all ears and promised to keep her conversation in confidence. He drew closer so that her bodyguard could not hear what was being said. She lowered her voice almost to a whisper and began her story.

"First, let me say that I love my father and brother very much. I would never do anything that would hurt them or bring shame upon them. What I am telling you must never be repeated."

Timar could tell that she was unsure about him. Yet, he could also tell that she needed someone in which to confide her secrets and dreams. He was glad she was giving him the opportunity to listen.

She continued, "I have lived a happy life here on Wolf River with Tana-qate and my father. Until recently, I never understood why father was so protective of me. One night, I overheard a conversation between them, and then it all became clear to me.

Tana-qate was telling father he was ready to become a warrior. He is only seventeen years old, yet after much pleading, father agreed to let him go on a hunting trip with a group of other warriors. Tana-qate said he would prove himself worthy to be a warrior of the Shawnee people during the trip. He also said that when he returned, he wanted to take a wife. Not just any wife, but one that he had loved for many years. Father was surprised that his son was mature enough to be thinking about moving out of the family lodge and starting a family of his own.

At first, father seemed proud of Tana-qate and told him that marriage came with great responsibilities; that he must be sure of his intentions. He told father he was ready."

Telah suddenly became very nervous and allowed Timar to take her hand. He felt her shake as she returned to her story.

"My father asked him who the lucky girl might be and that is when I got the most terrible shock of my life. Tana-qate told him he was going to marry me! I couldn't believe what I was hearing. I love Tana-qate, but only as a brother. We have never been intimate, not even for one second. What kind of trick was he playing on my father, I thought?

It was then, that I heard another frightening comment. This time it came from my own father. He said, 'You have chosen well, my son.' I couldn't believe my ears. A brother does not marry his own sister. Anyone in our village would tell you that it is wrong and against the customs of our people.

Then it became more clear as father continued to speak. He told Tana-qate it was not often that a father was blessed to raise an adopted daughter to become the wife of an only son. I am still not over the shock of hearing those words. How could he not be my real father? I have been his daughter for as long as I can remember."

Tears were starting to run down her lovely face and Timar tried to comfort her by touching her cheek to wipe them away. She looked into his eyes as he took her face in both hands and held it until she regained her composure. She tried to continue, but he put his finger to her lips and told her to rest for a moment.

When she realized Timar was holding her, she resisted his touch and stepped back a few feet. She suddenly realized that she had a strange feeling which permeated her whole body. Never had she felt like this before.

"I must be going," she said. When she reached the door, Telah entreated him to keep his word. "I have your word that you will never tell anyone what I just told you."

Timar nodded and remained silent as he watched her leave. What she told him was causing his head to spin. It was at that moment he realized he must never let her marry Tana-qate. He was in love with this beautiful girl himself.

She came again next afternoon, looking fresh and pretty as a wild mountain rose, dressed in a beautiful white doeskin dress. Timar greeted her with a big smile, as she took her seat beside his bed.

"Looks like you're going somewhere," said Timar, noticing that she was dressed differently than all the times he'd seen her.

"I am going nowhere. This is my wedding dress. I am returning from a friend's lodge, where she spent many hours on this dress in preparation for my marriage," replied Telah.

Timar felt a pang of anxiety flood his heart. He wanted to tell her how he felt, but realized he was in no position to interfere with the inevitable. After all, he was an outsider- practically a prisoner of the Shawnees and she had no business knowing what had been going on in his mind since the first time he laid eyes on her.

"I came to tell you that this will be my last visit. Tana-qate has already expressed his intentions to me and said it would not be right for me to continue seeing you," she said without looking up.

"Then, you plan to marry Tana-qate?" asked Timar. He wanted her to tell him differently.

"I do not wish to marry him, but I cannot go against my father's wishes. Oh, Timar, if there was any other way, I would take it," she started sobbing.

He tried to comfort her by saying, "I'm sure your father wants what is best for you."

"I must tell you what I learned today from the older friend who made this dress. When I told her who I was marrying, she said she already knew; that she had known for years of my father's plan. I told her about overhearing father and Tana-qate. She then told me the whole story of my life," said Telah, wiping the tears from her eyes.

Timar was anxious to learn more and leaned closer. Telah did not resist when he took her hands and held them. He could see the saddness come over her face as she continued.

"Sixteen summers ago, father led a war party south to deal with the Cherokees who were encamped along the Clinche River, many days from here. They were successful in attacking them and pushing the survivors of the battle out of Shawnee lands. Many Cherokees were killed, including some of their women. My real father and mother were, unfortunately, killed in the attack. When the battle was over, they discovered a baby girl, hidden in one of the wigwams. My father brought the little survivor home with him and adopted her into his family, giving her the Shawnee name, Telah," she related.

"I've never known anything but the ways of the Wolf River Shawnees. They are my family and I will always love them for raising me. That is one of the reasons I cannot marry Tana-qate. He is my brother and will always be," she cried.

Timar took the opportunity to speak.

"If you do not wish to marry Tana-qate, would you be upset if I told you there may be a way out of the problem?" he asked her.

"Why would I be upset? If you have an answer for my

problem. I'd like to hear it," she replied

"Well, you might not agree with me, but I'll tell you what I feel and how I think you will get out of the marriage with Tana-qate. I want you to know that since I've been here, I've grown to respect you for taking my interests to heart. No one else took the effort to look out for me as you did," said Timar.

"It was you who helped me get through the gauntlet. I heard your voice urging me on and it gave me the strength to finish the run. It was you who took the time to check on my wounds and watch over me while I recovered. No one else has ever done so much for me," he said, still holding her hands in his.

Timar could see that she cared. Her eyes told him that she had deep feelings for him, as he continued. "There is only one way that you can get out of marrying Tana-qate and that is to leave Wolf River."

"But, how is that possible? I have never been anywhere else. My father would never let me leave," she said.

"I can help," said Timar. "If you will let me, I will see that you do not have to go through with the marriage."

"How is it possible for you to help me?" she asked. "You are practically confined here with Tilpa and Mistha, and being watched closely by others in the village."

"That is true. They watch me closely during the day, but what they don't know is that I've been going outside the village at night after everyone's asleep. Each night, I have ranged farther, marking a trail that I will use when I escape," he said.

She understood what he was trying to tell her. "You mean you want me to escape with you?"

"Yes," said Timar. "I know that is the only way you will be free from Tana-qate.

Telah was unsure what to say. She was shocked to hear that Timar had been leaving the village at night, not because of him planning an escape, but because she saw the danger of him being caught. She knew how her father would react to his escape. Others had tried and been put to death for their effort.

"It is too dangerous. My father would catch us and you

would be tortured and killed," she cried. "I would rather marry Tana-qate than cause you to be put to death trying to help me."

"Then, you do have feelings for me." he said, trying to calm her. "I have wished it since the first time I saw you."

She could not contain the thoughts swirling through her head. Her first reaction was to get up and leave, but when she felt Timar pull her toward him, she submitted. His lips found hers and suddenly she was in his arms.

The following moments were filled with emotions neither of them had ever felt. The kiss lasted no more than a few seconds, but confirmed what both of them wanted the other to know. In silence, he held her close for several minutes, then releasing her, he held her face close and looked into her beautiful dark eyes.

"You cannot do something your heart tells you is wrong," he said pleadingly. "You must let your father know that you don't want to marry Tana-qate. If he is the father I think he is, he will understand and change Tana-qate's mind."

"I have already pleaded with him. He says only Tana-qate can change his mind. He is happy that his son has chosen me," she replied, with tears beginning to run down her cheeks.

"There is one way that I can keep him from taking you," said Timar. "According to your own tribal traditions, a man can challenge another, if there is a dispute. I will certainly make it known to your brother that I challenge him for the right to marry you. Your father will have to agree with the challenge; the council will see to that."

"No! No! You cannot challenge Tana-qate. He is just a boy. If you took his life, my father would have you killed also," she cried. "I would lose both, you and my brother. There must be a better way."

Timar took her in his arms and held her tightly. He could feel her trembling and tilted her face upward, gently placing a kiss on her lips.

"There is only one way," he said, "I want you to leave this place with me."

"Oh, Timar, I don't know what to do," she cried.

"We have some time yet. Why don't you think about it," he said. "If you decide to leave with me, we will need to make some preparations."

She quietly slipped out of his arms, touching his face as she stepped backward. He let her go without saying another word.

News of the wedding came the following day as Tana-qate, himself, announced it to the Wolf River council of elders. None of them objected when he told them of his plan to marry Telah. They were already aware of the situation, having been told by Black Fish, who proudly entreated them to agree with his son's wishes.

The whole village knew about the wedding within a few minutes after he met with the council. Tana-qate and his young friends ran through the village announcing his wedding to Telah. The ceremony was to take place in a week in the main longhouse with everyone being invited.

Timar heard the news from Tilpa and Mistha. They came running to tell him that his daily visitor was getting married to Tana-qate. Over and over they repeated the announcement until Timar could stand it no more. He left them still talking to each other and walked out of their lodge to find solitude near the edge of the village.

He had already made the decision to escape. Whether he would be going alone, he didn't know. He wanted to take Telah with him, but that was her decision to make.

Timar did not see her for two whole days. She did not come by to check on him as she normally did in the afternoons. He was worried that her father was overly protecting her by keeping her confined to quarters until the wedding. He missed her visits and wondered if she were feeling the same emptiness he felt deep in his heart.

He paced the floor of the lodge like a caged rat, until Tilpa finally asked, "What causes Timar to be uneasy today?" Before he could answer, she went on to say, "You have not eaten your food. Do you not like what we fix for you?"

"Oh, I guess I'm not very hungry today," he replied. "You and Mistha have been good to me. I thank both of you for all you have done. I guess I'm getting bored, being cooped up and unable to spend much time outside."

He tried to ease their worrying about him, knowing they had noticed a change in his normal daily routine. Timar stopped his pacing and returned to sit on his bed, hoping they were not somehow aware of his plan to escape. He decided to be more careful around the two women, since they were probably reporting his every move to Black Fish.

The day passed without a visit from Telah. If she didn't come tomorrow, he would go ahead with his plan to escape without her.

Chapter Twenty-Five
Escape from Wolf River

On the third day after his last talk with Telah, Timar rose early to set his escape plan in motion. While Tilpa and Mistha were preparing breakfast, he retrieved his pack from beneath his bed and checked the contents one last time. He had been saving back a few morsels each time they brought him food, slipping it into the pack without them seeing him, keeping it until the day when he made his escape from the village.

This morning seemed different than the preceding ones. He guessed it was because it would be his last day with the Shawnees. At least, that was his thought as he walked to the latrine area behind the main longhouse.

After he'd relieved himself, he started to return to his quarters when he felt something hit the back of his head. Stopping to investigate, he saw that someone had tossed a small stone from the direction of the adjacent lodge near the longhouse. He stood there for a few moments, waiting to see who was trying to get his attention.

In the dark shadows behind the lodge, he saw a movement. Then he saw a small hand motioning for him to come. He immediately knew who it was and ran toward the shadows.

"I am sorry that I was not able to visit you," she said, melting into his arms. "They watch my every move. Tana-qate is suspicious. He has not let me out of his sight for two days."

"I have missed you," said Timar. "I love you, Telah. I don't think I could live if you married Tana-qate."

"I know, my love. That is why I have decided to leave with you," she whispered.

Timar was so happy to hear her say she loved him. He kissed her over and over until she became so weak that she could hardly stand. When he finally released her, she spoke softly into his ear.

"They have set the time for the wedding. It is to take

place at noon tomorrow."

"Then we must leave tonight," said Timar. "We need the darkness to help cover our escape. Do you think you can do some things for me before then?"

"Yes, my love. I'll do whatever you wish," she said.

"First, we will need to be dressed for the cold. Can you manage to get my winter coat and boots?" he asked.

"I know where they have stored them, along with your rifle and pack. It will be easy to get them since the building is unguarded. Where should I leave them?"

"Why not leave them right here? We can meet here before we leave. Do you think you can be ready by midnight?" he asked.

"I'm ready to go now, but I know we wouldn't get far in the daylight," she smiled. "Is there anything else? I've got to get back before I'm missed."

"Just wear something warm and pray that we will be able to leave without being seen," he whispered, kissing her one last time.

After they separated, Timar returned to his living quarters, feeling elated that Telah was going to escape with him. He knew she must love him very much to leave everything she'd ever known for a man who was taking her far away from her family.

The day finally came to an end. It was the longest day of Timar's life, as he tried to keep the secret of his escape to himself. He spent the day thinking of the trail back to the Clinche Mountains and how hard it was going to be on Telah. She was going to be with him and he would take care of her, he thought, vowing to protect her with his life.

After the evening meal, Timar thanked the two women who doted over him. He appreciated them for taking him into their home, but it would soon be over. In a way, he would miss their mothering, and he was sure they would miss tending to the strange Seneca boy who had come into their lives.

Telah was waiting when he got there. She was dressed in dark buckskin pants and shirt, covered with a heavy buffalo overcoat. He was glad to see that she'd had no trouble slipping away from her family. They kissed and held each other for a few minutes.

"Are you sure?" asked Timar. "You will never see your family again."

"I'm sure I want to be with the man I love," she replied.

"Then, let's be on our way," he said.

He donned his winter coat and shouldered his pack, which she brought earlier. He checked the rifle, primed the pan and felt to see if the flint was positioned properly. Then silently, they slipped past the last building on the edge of the village and melted into the dark forest.

Timar told her they would have a few hours head start on Tana-qate and his warriors; that they would not miss them until daylight when the village awakened.

"We will need to be as far from the village as we can before sunrise," he told her. "I know it will be hard on you, but we must not let them catch up to us."

"I will keep up," she replied. "I will not let Tana-qate catch us."

They crossed the mountain range south of the village and were nearly twenty miles from the Shawnee village before the sun greeted them. Telah proved to be stronger than Timar realized. She kept up with his every step as they traveled without stopping, until he finally decided to let her rest a few minutes. When she told him she was ready to resume, they pushed onward.

Before darkness overtook them, they were back in familiar territory. Timar recognized the river crossing, where he and Sequah had crossed on their way to find Josh and Tobahana. They were making good time and he was surprised to find that she was able to keep up with him. At the river, they stopped and ate from the food she took from her family's table the night before. They ate corn cakes and washed them down with a drink from the river.

"If we can make it for two more days, we will be out of Shawnee lands," said Timar. "I know where we are. I crossed the river here, when my friend and I came looking for my brother."

"I know we'll make it, Timar. Now that I'm with you, I know you can get us to safety," she replied, snuggling closer to him.

They were still twenty miles or more from the big gorge. After wading across the river, Timar kept them heading south, along the trail which would eventually bring them to the entrance of the gorge. Of all the places he dreaded, the gorge was the most likely place they would find trouble. Beside traversing large boulders and climbing around sheer dropoffs, they would have to keep an eye out for Tana-qate and his warriors, who were also familiar with the gorge.

"We've got to keep going," said Timar. "I'd like to stop for the night so we could get some sleep, but he would surely overtake us. Another night and day will put us within shouting distance of my family's home, if we keep going."

"Whatever you say, Timar. I can keep up," she assured him.

Throughout the night, they worked their way upriver toward the big gorge which represented the dividing line between the territory of Kentuckee and the Virginia colony. Twenty miles of hard walking and climbing found them close to the northern entrance to the gorge. Timar cautioned Telah to be careful and not get too close to the roaring river, which sprayed them with a cold morning mist which froze to their faces and clothes. The rocks and cliffs along the stream were covered with a white sheet of ice, where the spray had frozen, causing them to slow down. They inched along the edge of the stream, slipping often on the slick stones.

Up ahead, the gorge narrowed and the noise increased to a deafening roar that blotted out all other noise. They were unable to hear each other's voice in the roaring of the white water. Timar held Telah's hand tightly as he pulled her over one boulder after another, slowly rounding the first bend in the gorge.

Somewhere up ahead was the cave where he and Sequah discovered the dead Shawnee braves. When they reached it, he would use the cave to get some much needed rest before continuing through the gorge. He was sure that Telah was frozen to the bone. The front of her small face was covered with icicles which hung from the hood of her coat. More icicles streamed from her nose, eyes and chin. Wiping the ice from his own face, he knew he had to stop and let her warm up if they could make it to the cave.

The sound of a rifle shot echoed through the gorge as a bullet spanged off the stone behind them.

"They're above us!" he shouted. "We've got to find cover."

He pulled her behind the nearest boulder and hugged her close. "There's a cave just ahead of us. If we can get there, maybe we can keep them from shooting at us."

Timar watched the small puff of white smoke as it rose into the air and dissipated above the rim of the gorge, a thousand feet above them. The distance was too great to see how many warriors Tana-qate had brought with him. He guessed it was a large number, since they were on a mission to bring Telah back.

One thing was in their favor; Tana-qate would not allow his braves to shoot close to them for fear of hitting Telah. Timar knew he would soon be sending his warriors down into the gorge where they could easily overpower him and take Telah. He decided to make a break for the cave, where he could protect her and defend them against the coming threat.

"Let's go," he said, pulling her upright. "We've got to get to the cave."

She obeyed and followed closely behind Timar as he scrambled over the stony river bank. Another warning shot rang out; the bullet hitting a boulder fifty feet in front of them. He pushed harder, pulling her with him, until he could see the small entrance to the cave a hundred feet above them. No more shots came as they scrambled up the side of the gorge. Both of them reached the entrance at the same time and dove into the darkness of the small cavern.

"Stay near the back of the cave," he told her. "Watch out for the two dead Shawnee warriors laying against the back wall. They were there when Sequah and I visited the cave on our trip into Kentuckee."

"Who are they?" she asked.

"I think they were killed by my brother when Tana-qate was taken prisoner," replied Timar.

"I don't want to look at them," she said. "I would know their faces."

He said no more to her for several minutes, allowing her to become accustomed to the darkness of the cave. She crawled close to him and lay quietly by his side. He drew her closer to him and they waited for Tana-qate to make his next move.

Timar saw them descending the gorge directly across from their cave. More than a dozen warriors, with their rifles and bows strung across their backs, were slowly climbing down the stone cliffs. He knew they would be closing in on the cave soon after they crossed the stream.

He guessed the distance across the stream to the descending climbers was nearly two hundred yards. It was not as far as the longest shot he'd ever made, so he brought his longrifle into position at the cave entrance and sighted on the nearest warrior. He aimed directly at the Shawnee's head and touched the set trigger. White smoke rolled from the gun barrel and pan. When it cleared, he saw the warrior lying on the rocks at the bottom of the gorge.

Timar watched his hands shake as he worked eagerly to reload. He had just taken his first life.

Within seconds, he reloaded and took aim at the next warrior. The rifle ball caught the brave midway of his back and he released his hold on the rocky cliff. His body crashed into the stones near the first brave. Several of the Shawnee climbers scrambled back up the face of the gorge as Timar reloaded his rifle.

He saw two of them make it to the river bed and take

hiding positions behind boulders. This time, he had them pinned down on the other side of the river; at least for a while, until he fired his next shot. Then they would get across the river while he was reloading.

"Looks like a stalemate, at least for a while," he told Telah. "As long as they stay hidden, I can't shoot. If I shoot, they will be across the river before I can stop them."

He kept his rifle trained on the location of the two hidden warriors. He knew he could take one of them if they decided to rush the cave. So he waited.

It was getting late in the afternoon; shadows were already streaming across the eastern side of the gorge, making it hard for Timar to see in the darkness around the overhangs. He knew it was just a matter of time until they rushed the cave. They knew he had only one rifle and could only kill one of their number if they rushed him. Time was on Tana-qate's side. He could wait until darkness and bring all of his warriors across the river without losing a man.

Timar and Telah had been without sleep for more than two days, now. They were tired and hungry and cold since the flight from the village. He fought hard to keep his eyes open as he watched the boulders across the stream. His eyes started to play tricks on him, as shadows danced on the water below. Soon, it would be all over.

He thought of how his life could have been with Telah as his wife. She was what he'd been hoping to find. She would have been the perfect mate for for him. Even Meriah would have approved of Telah and would have been proud of her young brother for fighting to keep her.

His thoughts of Telah were interrupted when suddenly the two warriors jumped from their concealment and rushed toward him. He touched off the rifle and saw one of them fall headlong into the stream. The other warrior made it across unscathed and quickly started climbing up the embankment toward the cave. He handed Telah the rifle and drew his knife for the fight that was sure to come quickly.

The warrior's head appeared at the cave entrance and in a flash, he was inside, swinging his tomahawk at Timar. He lunged forward, sending the blade of the tomahawk singing past Timar's head. Timar ducked and lunged into the Shawnee brave with all his strength, causing both of them to fall onto the floor of the cave. The warrior jumped quickly to his feet and circled the young Seneca, grinning as he tossed the sharp weapon from hand to hand.

Timar waited until he saw the tomahawk leave his right hand and quickly thrust his knife forward. It cut deeply into the warriors right hand, leaving him with only his left hand to hold the tomahawk. Blood ran in spurts from the knife wound and the warrior glanced down to see the damage. That was his only mistake. Timar took a chance and stepped toward the brave, feeling the knife cut through flesh and go deeply into the Shawnee's chest. He fell forward with a surprised stare on his face.

Timar quickly reloaded his rifle and took his position at the entrance of the cave. Telah joined him and lay beside him. They watched the other side of the gorge for signs of Tana-qate's warriors.

"Its just a matter of time," said Timar. "He knows it will be dark soon. He won't risk losing another warrior during the daylight hours. All he has to do is wait."

"Then, we will wait together," said Telah. "I will not let Tana-qate take me back. We will die together when the time comes."

"You must not," said Timar. "You've got to go back. I'd rather see you married to Tana-qate than see you die ."

"I cannot, my love. Life would not be worth living without you. Tana-qate would make my life so miserable that I would not want to live even one minute as his wife," she sobbed.

"We will die together, then," said Timar, holding her trembling body close.

He handed her the knife he'd used on the Shawnee warrior. "When the time comes, I will use the Shawnee's knife.

They lay together at the entrance of the cave and watched

the shadows climb the wall of the gorge on the other side of the stream. They talked about their childhood and the things that made them laugh. She asked about his family and learned of his life on Josh Mosby's farm in a little valley south of the Painted Mountain, which he also told her about.

The shadows were reaching the top of the gorge and the darkness was creeping into the area, making it hard for them to see the cliffs on the other side of the stream. Timar knew they were probably already descending the heights, but couldn't see any movement. Just then, he saw a warrior wade into the stream, holding his rifle over his head. Then two more joined him in the water.

Timar touched the set trigger and watched the first brave hit the water. He couldn't believe his eyes when the other two Shawnees threw up their arms and fell into the swirling stream. As several Shawnees reached the bottom of the gorge, two more were sent sprawling onto the rocks. Timar heard the echo of rifles booming through the gorge and quickly began reloading his own rifle.

He could hear his name being called from somewhere above him and shouted loudly that he was in the cave. He knew if it was Tobahana and Josh, they would know just where he was. A broad smile crossed his face as he took aim at another Shawnee brave and fired.

Rifles boomed again overhead and two more unfortunate souls went to the spirit world. Then it was all over. No more shots were fired.

Timar drew Telah to him and they stood in the entrance of the cave and waited. He told her they had been saved by his brother and Josh Mosby, who would be joining them shortly.

They came down the wall of the castle-like spire and were met at the cave entrance by Timar. Tobahana was the first to greet his little brother, grabbing him in a bear hug that took the wind out of him. Josh entered next and gave Timar a huge slap on the back, followed by another hug.

Telah stood shyly to one side, unnoticed as they greeted

each other. Timar told them there was someone he wanted them to meet. They turned to see the girl standing there.

"This is Telah," he said proudly taking her by the hand. "She is the daughter of Chief Black Fish. And, no, she is not my prisoner. She is going to be my wife."

"Glad to meet you, Telah," they both said at the same time.

She smiled and shyly extended her free hand. "I am Telah, no longer daughter of Chief Black Fish. I am glad to know the brother and brother-in-law of Timar, who will soon be my husband."

They left the gorge at first light. No one wanted to know whether Tana-qate had lived through the fight. They didn't bother to look at the bodies of the fallen Shawnee warriors and left them where they lay along the river bank.

It took another day before the little cabin of Josh Mosby came into view. Timar was happy to see the place where he'd spent the last ten years of his life. He couldn't wait to see the smile on Meriah's face, knowing she would be pleased to meet his Telah.

She was waiting at the creek as they rounded the last bend. Meriah waded the stream and ran to meet them. Timar broke away from the others and rushed to see his sister, who met him with open arms.

"Oh, Timar, my brother. We thought we had lost you," she shouted.

"Only for a short while," he said as he lifted her off her feet with a big hug.

"Someone else comes with Josh and Tobahana," she said, noticing the small figure walking between them.

"Yes," he said. "It is someone I want you to welcome into our family."

When they reached Meriah and Timar, Josh gave her a kiss and hug, followed by one from Tobahana. She told them she was glad they all made it back safely.

Timar then introduced her to Telah, who held tightly onto his hand.

"This is Telah. She was the daughter of the chief of the Wolf River Shawnees. She is going to be part of our family," he said. "Telah is going to be my wife."

"Oh, Timar," Meriah cried. "She is beautiful."

Forgetting that she failed to properly introduce herself, Meriah said. "I am Meriah, Timar's sister, wife of Josh Mosby and sister to Tobahana of the Senecas."

She took Telah's hand and walked beside her toward the cabin as the evening sun peeked through the clouds and touched the Clinche Mountain, south of the little valley.

EPILOGUE

The frontier of America in the 1700's produced many legendary men who became our heroes and have spread their influence even into the twenty-first century. Men such as Daniel Boone, John Finley, and Simon Kenton will be remembered as the forerunners for all those who followed their dreams in the exploration of new lands. In this novel, I have tried to portray them as ordinary men who were caught up in the extraordinary time of expansion in colonial America.

Daniel Boone

Referencing his book, I used Daniel Boone's own words describing his first trip into Kentucky. It was written before he died in 1820 on his daughter, Jemima's, farm in Missouri. He tells of his capture by the Shawnee chief, Black Fish and his escape to meet his brother, Squire Boone, later. They stayed the winter in Kentucky, where they explored the region and hunted game for two more years before returning home. He falls in love with the beautiful Kentucky scenery and vows to return with his family.

Boone returns in October, 1773 and is met at the Cumberland Gap by the Shawnees, who attacked his party. His oldest son, James, was killed in the incident, causing him to give up and return home.

Finally, in 1775, he successfully brought his wife, Rebecca and family to Kentucky, where he established the settlement of Boonesborough. A year later, he rescued his daughter, Jemima, and two other girls from the Shawnees. He is captured by the Shawnees in 1778 and after escaping some four months later, he rejoined his family who had returned to North Carolina.

Boone's son, Israel, was killed at Blue Lick, Kentucky, while attacking the Shawnees. Daniel was one of the commanding officers in the Kentucky Militia. Colonel Boone moves his family to Ohio in 1783, where he led raids on Shawnee settlements.

Boone served on the Virginia Assembly several times, promoting the migration of settlers to the west. He relocated his family to Missouri after disputes over land grants and indebtness and tried to get a Spanish land grant, which was rejected in 1809. Boone lost his faithful wife, Rebecca in 1813 and received a tract of land in Missouri as a gift from the U.S. Government in 1814. At the age of 86, Daniel Boone died on the 26th of September, 1820 in Missouri.

John Finley

Frontiersman John Finley was an immigrant, born in Ireland in 1706 who came to America with his father when he was a small boy. John Finley was not new to Kentucky, having led a successful hunting expedition into Kentucky in 1767. He was familiar with the Shawnees, who allowed him to take game. However, he was told not to return. In May, 1769, at the age of 63, he led another hunting party down the Ohio River and into Kentucky. With him were Daniel Boone and four other hunters who were captured at the place called Blue Lick. John Finley was killed by the Shawnees in Virginia in 1773.

Simon Kenton

Perhaps the most famous of the longknives was Simon Kenton. Born in Prince William County, Virginia in 1755, he was destined to become one of the most colorful personalities of the American Frontier. As a young boy of 15, he fell in love with Ellen Cummins, who spurned him, and married one of the Leachman boys. At the wedding, young Simon called Willie Leachman out, and was nearly beaten to death by his cronies. A year later, Kenton found Leachman working in the woods and beat him mercilessly. He believed he had killed Leachman, so he lit out for the wilderness to escape the authorities. He changed his name to Simon Butler over the incident; a name which he wore for nine years, until he found out that Leachman was alive.

He became friends with Daniel Boone and hunted with him on several trips along the frontier. Simon was captured by the Shawnees more than once and forced to run the gauntlet seven different times. Once, trying to escape from the gauntlet, he was hit in the head by a Shawnee war club, which left a gaping hole in his head. Unconscious for three days, he survived the blow and eventually escaped again. He was burned at the stake by the Shawnees on three occasions and still lived through their torture. During his last capture, he escaped stark-naked in the dead of winter and outran the Shawnees for two hundred miles before reaching safety. It is said that Simon Kenton was the only man who was strong enough to take all the punishment the Shawnees could give, and still live through it.

On April 24, 1777, in a battle with the Shawnees near Boonesborough, Kenton saved the life of his old friend, Daniel Boone. They fought together against the Shawnees on numerous occasions, until Kenton left Kentucky and moved to the Ohio country. During the American Revolution, he fought against the British and Indians, with his friend, George Rogers Clark, along the Ohio River. In 1805, he received a promotion to brigadier general in the Ohio militia.

Kenton lived out his remaining years along the Ohio River and died in 1836. A monument was erected in Urbana, Ohio in 1884, to memorialize this great longknife of the American Frontier.

Black Fish

The Shawnee chief, Black Fish was one of Daniel Boone's archenemies. Many times, he attacked the settlements in Kentucky, trying to keep the white settlers out of his hunting grounds. He captured Daniel Boone on one occasion, adopting him into his village. But after three months, Boone saw his opportunity and escaped in the dead of night. Black Fish and his Shawnee forces were repelled in the attack against Boonesborough in 1777.

Amos Boggs
 A purely fictional character, who was typical of the hearty men who served as scouts for the British Army during the migration of settlers in the 1770's. Although Boggs is portrayed as somewhat of a scoundrel, the times dictated their conduct. He represents the old scout, full of indignation toward the British, yet accepts their pay and benefits.

The Gorge
 The gorge is real. It lies on the border between Virginia and Kentucky. Today, it is main attraction of the Breaks Interstate Park. Its scenery is breathtakingly beautiful and appears as it did two hundred years ago, with the exception of the railway and tunnel along the Russell Fork River far below the rim of the gorge. It is viewed with awe as one of the most beautiful strokes of the Masters Hand.